HELLO!
Welcome to Louie's book. You can turn the page now.

by **JENNY MEYERHOFF**

with pictures by **JASON WEEK**

Farrar Straus Giroux ◦ New York

Farrar Straus Giroux Books for Young Readers
175 Fifth Avenue, New York 10010

Printed in the United States of America by
RR Donnelley & Sons Company, Harrisonburg, Virginia
Designed by Andrew Arnold
First edition, 2013
1 3 5 7 9 10 8 6 4 2

mackids.com

Library of Congress Cataloging-in-Publication Data

Meyerhoff, Jenny.
The barftastic life of Louie Burger / Jenny Meyerhoff; pictures by Jason Week. — 1st ed.
p. cm.
Summary: With a school Talent Bonanza coming up, there is only one thing that can keep fifth-grader Louie Burger from taking a big step toward his dream of becoming a world-famous comedian—extreme stage fright.
ISBN 978-0-374-30518-5 (hardcover)
ISBN 978-0-374-30519-2 (e-book)
[1. Comedians—Fiction. 2. Stage fright—Fiction. 3. Family life—Fiction. 4. Friendship—Fiction. 5. Schools—Fiction. 6. Talent shows—Fiction. 7. Humorous stories.] I. Week, Jason, ill. II. Title.
PZ7.M571753Bar 2013
[Fic]—dc23

2012029524

Farrar Straus Giroux Books for Young Readers may be purchased for business or promotional use. For information on bulk purchases please contact Macmillan Corporate and Premium Sales Department at (800) 221-7945 x5442 or by email at specialmarkets@macmillan.com.

For
Sarah, Donnie, Dave, Joe, and Ben

I didn't get to choose you, but
I would have if I could.

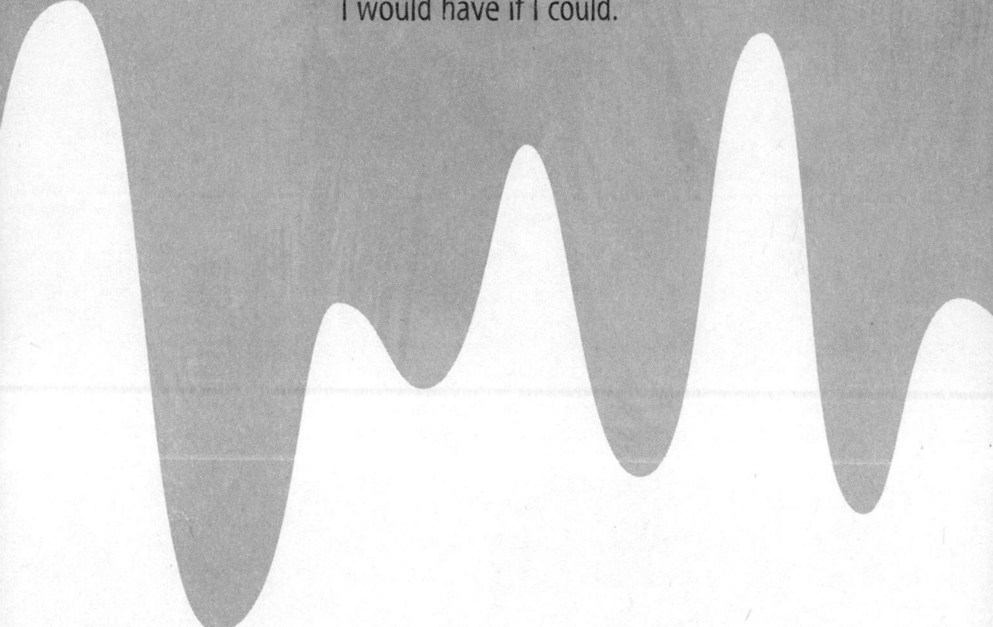

THE BARFTASTIC
LIFE
OF
LOUIE
BURGER

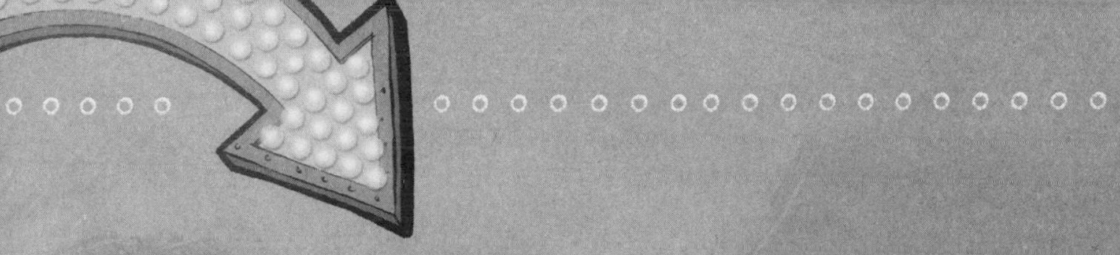

NOSTRIL HAIR

I step into my closet, which is twice the size of my bedroom, and flick the special switch my dad installed. Footlights glow in the corners of the room and along the edge of the built-in stage. My arms tingle.

"Laaadies and gennntlemen!" the announcer's voice booms inside my head. "Put your hands together for the next act in the fifth-grade talent show . . . Looooou-ie Burrrrr-ger!"

I jog onto the stage, grab the microphone, and toss it from my left hand to my right.

"Thank you. Thank you," I say. "It's great to be here in the Barker Elementary gym, but don't ask me to do any pull-ups. I had to do pull-ups for the

President's Challenge fitness test, and I sprained my armpit. I guess I'll never be president."

I pause for a minute to let the crowd laugh. Today the crowd is made up of shoes, T-shirts, and posters of my favorite comedians, especially my idol, Lou Lafferman.

I'm about to deliver my bit about school

cafeterias when I hear a knock at the door, and my dad bursts in. Instantly I feel naked with nothing but a microphone stand to hide behind. I dive off the stage, land in my beanbag chair, and grab a *Nutso* magazine.

Dad raises an eyebrow. My magazine is upside down. I toss it on the floor and fold my arms across my chest. "You're supposed to wait until I say come in."

"Sorry. I forgot." He steps back outside and knocks again.

I roll my eyes. "Come in."

Dad slips inside, sits on the floor, and smiles at me. "I'm glad you're using the stage. Are you ready to show me your act?"

"Not yet." I squirm. "It's not finished."

Seriously. I've only been working on it for two years. You can't rush comedy.

My dad nods slowly, and I blush. There's one problem with my dream of becoming a world-famous comedian. I'm too chicken to show anyone my act. What's the deal with stage fright? It's not like the stage is going to bite me or give me a wedgie. It would make more sense to have *audience* fright.

Actually, I have that, too.

I slump off the beanbag and onto the floor. "Sorry you wasted your time building the stage."

Dad made me the coolest stage any kid has ever had in his closet: shiny black, with neon silhouettes of laughing people painted around the sides. There's a silver curtain for the backdrop, too, exactly like the one on *Lou Lafferman's Laff Nite*. It took us three whole days to make, and I didn't even have to ask for it. Dad heard me mention how cool it would be to have a stage like Lou's, how it would make me feel like a real comedian, and *boom*, next thing you know, we're building a stage.

Dad squeezes my shoulder. "I'm glad we built it. I bet now that you have the stage, you'll be ready to perform for an audience in no time. Maybe if my parents had pushed me when I was your age, I would already be a successful artist, instead of a forty-year-old beginner."

When he says that, he stares right into my eyes. A funny feeling burbles in the pit of my stomach, and I imagine my grandparents pushing my father off the roof of their house with one of his sculptures. It doesn't sound so great to me. My dad's a junk artist, by the way. That's a real thing. You can Google it.

"Sometimes kids need a push," he continues.

"Sometimes they need a forty-two-inch flat-screen TV in their bedroom."

My dad laughs, then nods his head as if he's decided something. "You're funny, Louie. You should do your act in the school talent show."

The mention of the show turns my intestines to Jell-O. "Uh, the show was canceled this year," I say.

"Nice try." Dad gives me a noogie. "But it was printed in black and white on the calendar that came with your class list last week. The show is next month, plenty of time for you to finish your act. It'll be good for you."

I picture myself standing in the spotlight, telling my jokes while Ryan Rakefield shouts from the back of the room, "You're so funny I forgot to laugh!" It's the same way he heckled me in third grade when I told knock-knock jokes for show-and-tell.

"Too many people," I say.

Dad nods his head sympathetically, and I sigh in relief. Then he says, "Start smaller. Do your act for *me*."

Even one person feels like too many. My dad might not laugh. A shoes, T-shirts, and baseball-cap crowd is much safer. "My throat's dry."

"I understand. Maybe another time." Dad gets

up and puts his hand on the doorknob. "Tomorrow's a big day. You nervous?"

Tomorrow is the first day of fifth grade. I should be nervous, since Ryan Rakefield is in my class. Again. But I actually feel excited about school this year because my best friend is finally in my class, too. Nick Yamashita. First time ever!

"Nah," I say. "Not with Nick in my class."

"I've got a big day tomorrow, too."

"You do?" I turn my head to look up at him. He has a lot more hair in his nostrils than I remembered. I bet it keeps his boogers warm.

"I'm meeting with a gallery owner."

"But Mom said it would be *years* before you start to sell your work."

My dad tilts his head and gives me a curious look. "She did?"

"Uh . . ." I scratch my head. I think that was supposed to be a secret.

Eight weeks ago my dad was a vice president of strategic marketing. Then his company decided they didn't need so many vice presidents. They gave him a pile of money, though, so Dad decided to try his dream of being an artist, and Mom decided to go back to work. She also gave Ariella, Ruby, and me a million talks about saving money, helping around the house, and being patient and supportive.

"No. Wait. I'm confused," I say to my dad. "I think she said *days*."

Dad rubs his left temple. I don't think he believes me, and I worry that what I said to him was the junk artist version of *You're so funny I forgot to laugh*. I want to take it back.

"Uh, Dad," I say before I can stop myself, "maybe I could do my act for you tomorrow. After school."

"You're on!" My dad's happiness almost cancels out the cold, clammy feeling spreading down my neck. He snaps his fingers. "Let's make a pact. I'll take the art world by storm, and you'll become a comedy showstopper."

My dad does jazz hands and Groucho Marx eyebrows as if to say *Whaddaya think?*

I'm not sure. I want to be a comedian more than

anything in the world, but what if . . . what if I'm not funny?

"Don't leave me hanging, Louie!" My dad clutches at his chest. "Let's help each other out tomorrow. The Burger men have to stick together."

"Okay," I say. "I'll try." I put out my hand, and my dad grabs it and shakes.

I hope I can live up to my end of the bargain.

The Barftastic Life of Louie Burger
A Comedy Sketchbook
By Louie Burger (obviously)

The Scientific Evidence That Proves I Am a Comedian

Exhibit A: I'm funny looking. I have curly orange hair. I'm skinnier than a jump rope and my ears stick out a mile. I'm also completely uncoordinated. Need I say more?
Exhibit B: I play the accordion.
Exhibit C: I'm strangely connected to many famous comedians. My initials are the same as Lucille Ball's. My birthday is the same as Charlie Chaplin's. And I'm from the same town as Bill Murray. Also, I have the same first name as Lou Lafferman, the greatest comedian in the history of comedians.
Exhibit D: I already have my own catchphrase: *barftastic!* It means *amazing* times *fantastic* plus *unbelievable.* Squared.

TOAST FOR DINNER

When we sit down for dinner, Dad pulls a bottle of sparkling apple cider out from under his seat. "I propose a toast!" he says.

Barftastic! Sparkling apple cider is one step away from soda. My mom doesn't usually let us have fizzy drinks.

Dad stands up, unscrews the cap, fills five wineglasses, and hands them out.

My mother laughs. "David, what is this about?"

"Tomorrow is a big day in the Burger household." Dad raises a glass. "To Mom's return to teaching high school gym."

We all take sips from our glasses, and bubbles fizz up my nose.

"To Ruby's first day of first grade." We start to take another sip, but Ruby interrupts us.

"Also, to my first day of changing my middle name to Butterflyunicornjokergirl and to my first day of greenish brown as my favorite color."

"To greenish brown." My dad nods as though Ruby said something normal. He claims Ruby marches to the beat of a different drummer, but if you ask me, she marches to the beat of a baked potato.

"This is so weird." Ari wrinkles her nose at the cider. She doesn't march to any beat. She stands on the sidelines and criticizes the drummer.

"To Ari's first day of middle school." Dad raises his glass. "We know you'll do great."

I gulp the rest of my cider and ask for a refill.

"To my new career," Dad says, passing me the bottle. When he finishes he holds his glass high. "To tomorrow's meeting at Trash Gallery!"

"Think of it as a trial run," Mom says. "The outcome doesn't matter."

Dad looks at my mom with a funny smile on his face, then he presses his lips together and shakes his head. "Thank you," he tells her, but his voice sounds annoyed.

"What's it Louie's first of?" Ruby asks, totally unaware that her question isn't grammatically correct.

"The first day of fifth grade is barely a first," Ari says. "It's the same as the first day of second, third, and fourth grade."

I stick my tongue out at her. She'd have

something bad to say even if it were my first day of being a superhero.

"Tomorrow is the world premiere of the comic stylings of Louie Burger. Louie is going to do his act for me!" My dad's words are for all of us, but he only looks at my mother as he speaks. "I'm going to do everything I can to support Louie's dream. To Louie's first performance!"

"To Louie!" Mom clinks her glass with Ruby and Ari.

"I want to watch from the front row of seats," Ruby says. "Can I?"

"Sorry," I tell her. "The show's sold out."

"Don't worry if your act doesn't go perfectly," Mom tells me as she sets her glass back down. "It's your first time. The very attempt already makes you a success in my eyes."

I want to remind her what Lou says about failure: *If at first you don't succeed, fail so spectacularly that everyone will think it's what you meant to do in the first place.* But my dad cuts me off.

"Louie's going to be great! In fact he's thinking about doing the fifth-grade talent show."

"I am?" I take another sip of cider, but the bubbles taste flat.

My mother looks back and forth between me and my father. "You don't have to do it if you don't feel ready, Louie."

"He'll be ready if we show him we believe in him," Dad replies.

"I don't think the talent show is a good idea." Ari shakes her head. "No one does comedy."

My mouth tastes sour from my last sip of cider. I wish we'd never toasted anything.

"That's not true, Ari," says my dad. "Two boys did Abbott and Costello's *Who's on First!* routine last year."

"Let me rephrase," says Ari. "People don't do their own lame jokes. People only do *real* comedy."

By real comedians. The kind who aren't afraid of audiences. Everyone at the table looks at me, and I shrink down in my chair.

"You are pushing him too hard," Mom tells my dad.

"I'm encouraging him. You are discouraging him."

My mother turns to me. "I'm sorry if it seems that way, hon. I don't mean to discourage you. Do you want to do the show?"

Ruby puts her hands over her ears. My dad folds his arms across his chest. Ari rolls her eyes.

I glance back and forth between my mom and my dad. "I'm not sure."

The room goes silent, and my mom gives my dad a look that says *See?*

Dad turns his fork over and over again in his hand. "What about our pact?"

"I thought that was about doing the act for you."

"Oh." He puts the fork down. "I guess I got ahead of you. But comedy is meant to be shared. You need to believe in yourself."

Dad sits back down in his seat and serves himself some salad.

"You don't need to decide tonight, Louie." My

mother serves herself salad, too, then passes the bowl to Ari. "Give yourself time. Maybe in a month you'll feel excited about being in the show."

"Maybe you'll be famous by then," says Ruby.

"Well, I still don't think you should make him do the talent show," says Ari, as she passes me the salad. I put seven cucumber circles on my plate, the only part of salad that I like. I can't decide if I should thank Ari or stick my tongue out at her again. It sounds like she's sticking up for me, but her words are an insult in disguise.

"What if I still don't want to?" I ask.

"Then you don't have to," my mother says. "We won't make you."

I look at my dad, but he doesn't say anything.

ooo

After dinner I head straight to my closet and step onto my stage. I can almost hear the applause and feel the warmth of the spotlights on my forehead. My shoulders relax and I smile.

"What's the deal with parents?" I begin. "They're

always pushing their kids. First they push them in a stroller, then they push them on a swing, then they push them to accomplish their dreams. If I ever pushed someone at school I'd get in trouble! 'Hey, Ryan, I think I should push you to be a little nicer.'" I pantomime shoving Ryan to the floor. "'And Principal Newton, I'd like to push you to buy a laptop for every student.'"

Around me, posters of famous comedians line the walls of my closet. I wonder if any of their parents had to push them. Probably not. I study each of my idols, and my eyes stop on the poster of Lou Lafferman standing in the spotlight with a circle of silver curtain glittering behind him. He's in the middle of a joke and his mouth is pulled down in an exaggerated frown. He looks the way I feel when I perform in my closet: in the zone. It's the way I can never imagine feeling in front of a real live audience.

"What do you think?" I ask Lou. I'm not crazy, by the way. I know he can't answer me. "If I do the talent show, will I kill or will I bomb?"

Also, by the way, in the world of comedy, killing is great but bombing stinks like the tuna sandwich you accidentally left in your lunch box over the entire summer vacation.

Lou's face stays in that funny frown, which I guess you could interpret either way. I sigh, turn off my microphone, and get ready for bed.

Barf Dictionary

Barfcredible (adj.): so good it makes you want to barf.

Barfnoying (adj.): really, really, really annoying. Ruby is *barfnoying.*

Barf-o-matic (n.): a machine I will invent someday that makes barfing sounds and shoots fake barf.

Barfomework (n.): boring pointless homework, meaning all homework.

Barforing (adj.): so boring it makes you want to barf.

Barforrible (adj.): so bad it makes you want to barf.

Barfshake (v.): to do the Barf Brothers' secret handshake. Only two people in the entire world know how to *barfshake.*

Barftastic (adj.): *amazing* times *fantastic* plus *unbelievable.* Squared.

Barftrocious (adj.): think of the worst thing you can imagine, and then add barf.

I AM NOT A UNICORN

"Louie! Ruby! Time for school! Hurry up! I have to leave soon, too, remember? I'm going downtown today!"

My dad's shouts are muffled through the closet door. I stop practicing my act and check the clock. Whoa! I don't even have time to brush my teeth. It'll be okay, though. I had Cocoa Puffs for breakfast—my breath smells nice and chocolaty. Normally, we are not allowed to have sugary cereals on weekdays, but Mom had to leave so early this morning, she wasn't here to enforce her rule.

"Ruby! Louie!" Dad shouts again. "Five minutes!"

I grab my school supplies and shove them into my backpack. Then I stare at my comedy journal, wondering if I should bring it to school, too. I'm about to throw the notebook into my backpack, when I notice there is something wrong with it.

On the cover, where it used to say The Barftastic Life of Louie Burger, it says this instead:

The Barftastic Life of Louie Burger
A Comedy Sketchbook
By Louie Burger (obviously)
and Ruby's unacorn Book
By butterflyunacornjokergirl

I have a feeling that's not the worst of it, so I peek inside.

best Unicrn Names
1. Sprakl
2. majik Star
3. Louie

That's plain wrong. Sometimes I wish Ruby would move to an island in the middle of the

Pacific Ocean and that after that boats and airplanes would be uninvented.

First, Louie is *not* a good unicorn name. Second, it's *my* notebook. Last, it was in a secret hiding place inside an old Parcheesi box. Ruby doesn't play Parcheesi. Last, part two, did I spell like that when I was in first grade?

"Five minutes are up! Nick and Henry are here!"

I race to the front door and see Nick and his little brother having a backpack war at the edge of our driveway. That's a game Nick and I invented. Nick swings his backpack at Henry in his signature move, the reverse double-strap swingback.

"Bye, Dad," I say, flinging the front door open. I can't wait to see Nick. I haven't seen him for five whole weeks. At the end of July, my family set out on a monthlong RV trip while Nick was being forced to attend sports camp and then, in August, Nick and his family went to visit his grandpa in Japan.

In kindergarten, first, second, third, and fourth

grades Nick and I were mostly at-home friends. Sure we'd see each other at recess, but we never got to be alone. The problem is, everyone likes Nick, and there were always lots of kids in his class who'd follow him outside. But this year, since I'll be in class with him, everyone will know he's *my* best friend. It's going to be the best fifth grade ever!

I'm halfway out the door to meet Nick when my dad puts a hand on my shoulder. "Hold on a minute."

For a second I worry that he's going to do something ridiculous like kiss me goodbye, but instead he asks, "Aren't you supposed to walk with your sister?"

"No way," I say. "Do you know what she did to my notebook?"

Dad rubs his chin. "I'll talk to her about the notebook later. Mom told me to make sure you walk with her. Do you know where she is?"

He should search outer space or the loony bin, since those are the two places she belongs. I'm about to suggest it when she clomps down the hallway. For the first day of school, Ruby is wearing a jack-o'-lantern turtleneck, *my* Hawaiian-print swimming trunks, *my Lou Lafferman's Laff Nite* hat, and cowboy boots.

"Da-ad!" I point at Ruby, but can't speak further.

Ruby. In my Lou Lafferman hat. That is as disrespectful as using an American flag as a diaper.

Dad wags a finger at Ruby. "You can't go into your brother's things without asking," he tells her.

"Sorry, Louie," she says. "I was nervous of first grade. I needed Louie power. Want a unicorn to trade?"

I sigh. My Lou hat is worth about a billion dollars. A unicorn is worth negative four cents. "Fine," I say. "You can give it back to me after school."

She walks out the door, and my dad bumps shoulders with me.

"That was nice," he says.

I shrug. I'm not letting her keep it forever, just for today.

"It's our big day. Wish me luck." Dad holds out his hand to me for a fist-bump.

I tap my knuckles against his. "Good luck," I say, and tear out the front door before he mentions my act. Maybe he'll forget about it by the end of the day.

I race down the driveway toward Nick. "Look out!" I scream as I run. "I'm going to hurl!"

When I'm inches away, I pretend to stick my index finger down my throat and so does Nick. Then we hook our fingers together and pull as hard as we can until they come apart and we fall on our butts. It's the Barf Brothers' secret handshake. We call ourselves the Barf Brothers because in second grade we finished an entire extra-large meat-lover's pizza at a sleepover and both threw up in our sleeping bags.

Nick stands and swings his backpack at me in a sideways packheader. I act dizzy for a second, and then I stand, too. Nick and I start walking, and Ruby and Henry trail along behind us. Close enough that they won't get lost, but far enough that hopefully no one will think we're together.

It's so great to see Nick again. Fifth grade is going to be barftastic.

POP

School can get a little lonely when you don't have a best friend in your class. A best friend always wants to be your partner and listens to your jokes. If you *don't* have a best friend in your class, everyone will think you are weird instead of hysterically funny when you put pencils in your nostrils because your nose went number two. Get it? *Number two* pencil.

Then Ryan Rakefield will tell everyone that you were trying to erase your boogers, and your classmates will call you the Invisible-Booger Boy for about a month. Um, I take it back. That didn't actually happen. *Really*.

Now that Nick is in my class, at least one person will get my jokes.

"School is going to be awesome this year," I tell Nick as we head down the sidewalk.

"Yeah," he says. "There are some cool kids in our class this year."

"Right," I say. "Us."

Nick laughs, but he also adds, "And other kids, too."

"Louie's going to be in the talent show," Ruby butts in from behind us. "He's going to be the star."

Nick stops walking and stares at me like he's trying to figure out if Ruby's telling the truth. "You're going to do your act?"

"No." I shake my head. "This is a misunderstanding."

"Too bad," he says.

I turn to Ruby. "Did you know that first graders who walk to school by themselves get five dollars from the principal?"

Ruby laughs. She doesn't start walking by herself.

I'm wondering if I should tell Nick about my performance for my dad when Henry bumps my elbow and wedges himself between Nick and me. "We went to see the Chunichi Dragons," he says.

We turn the corner onto the last block to school.

"Oooh. Dragons are cousins of unicorns," Ruby says.

"The Chunichi Dragons are a baseball team," Nick explains. "I got a ball signed by the players." He seems pretty excited about it, which is weird, since Nick and I have always agreed that sports are for snort-brains.

"We got dragon hats," Henry adds.

"Neat," I say. "I hope your hair doesn't get singed when it starts breathing fire."

Henry stares at me like he has no idea what I'm talking about.

"Naked mole rats aren't rats or moles," Ruby announces.

You never know what you're going to get with Ruby. Sometimes it's kind of fun, but I'm not in the mood for bizarre-animal-fact hour right now. "First kid to the corner wins an invisible pony!" I say. Ruby and Henry look at each other, then take off running.

"Nice one," Nick tells me when they're gone. "Wish I'd thought of that when I was in Japan. Henry kept butting in whenever my grandpa and

I tried to play catch. I learned how to throw a knuckleball, though. I'm going to do a pitching demonstration for the talent show."

Now it's my turn to stop walking. "A *pitching demonstration*? I thought we hated sports. You said sports camp would be a torture sundae with a tennis ball on top."

"*You* said that." Nick kicks a rock and it skitters to the end of the block, where Ruby, Henry, and the crossing guard wait for us. "It wasn't that bad."

We reach the corner and the crossing guard holds up the flashing stop sign that looks like an octagon-shaped Ping-Pong paddle. He escorts Nick, Ruby, Henry, and me to the other side of the street. Ruby and Henry race off to stand with the first graders, and Nick and I head to the other side of the blacktop. The closer we get to the fifth-grade area, the slower my feet move.

The fifth graders gather by the tetherball poles. Some are playing catch, some are standing around talking, but everyone is with a friend or group of friends. I look at Nick. He's walking with me, but he's a half step ahead. Our bodies aren't quite lined up.

And then I hear a voice.

"Hey, Nick. We're in the same class!"

I know that voice. A voice of pure evil. Ryan Rakefield.

Essential Backpack-War Moves*

Reverse double-strap swingback: Holding on to both straps, spin around 360 degrees counterclockwise and whack your opponent with your backpack.

Double-strap swingback: Same thing, only clockwise.

Backhack: Lift your backpack over your head until it touches your back, then hack it forward.

Single-strap X-attack: Holding on to one strap, swing your backpack in an X motion.

Zipper-zap: Snap the backpack forward and back so the zipper flaps out.

Stomachpack blast: Strap the pack onto the front of your body and blast your stomach forward.

Buttpack bomb: Holding on to both straps, swing your backpack up toward your opponent's butt.

Packheader: Backpack vs. head, enough said.

*Just make sure your backpack is filled with something soft, like a winter coat, when you play this game. Otherwise your friend might hit you someplace private with a pair of gym shoes in his bag and you'll have to walk the rest of the way home looking like the Hunchback of Notre Dame. Not that that actually happened. *Really.*

YOU CAN'T BE FRIENDS WITH A THERMOS

"Yamashita!" Ryan calls to Nick again. "Did you bring your football to school?"

I look at Nick, completely confused. Nick tightens the straps on his backpack, but he doesn't say anything until Ryan runs over and fake-tackles him.

"Hi, Ryan."

"You have to be on my team at recess this year," says Ryan. "Remember the day when you tackled me in the mud? That was so awesome. I don't understand why you never want to play with us. You're good. We could use you."

Nick nods, but I don't know if he's agreeing to play football or agreeing that knocking Ryan in the mud was awesome. It sounds awesome to me. I wish I remembered that day.

"Ryan was at sports camp with me," Nick explains.

Oh. Sports camp.

"It's the Invisible-Booger Boy!" Ryan pretend-punches me in the stomach, and I double over because I expect the punch to be real. "Gotcha!" he shouts.

Ryan bursts out laughing at his completely unfunny prank, and Nick rolls his eyes at me. I hope that means he still agrees with me about Ryan.

The bell rings and we follow Mrs. Adler into room thirteen, where she has the desks arranged in a big square with our names taped to our assigned places. Nick is next to me. Barftastic! Ryan is on my other side, but I'm going to pretend he's a desk lamp.

When we are seated, Mrs. Adler hands each student a bag of Hershey's Kisses. "To get the year off to a sweet start," she says.

"Gross," I whisper. "The teacher kissed us."

"Ewww!" shouts Ryan. "Mrs. Adler kissed us."

Everyone laughs. Including Mrs. Adler. At *my* joke.

"I know who'll be providing the comic relief this year," Mrs. Adler says, smiling at Ryan. He stands up and takes a bow. I should slide a whoopee cushion onto his seat, but unfortunately I forgot to bring one to school today.

If Ryan knew anything, he'd know that real

comedians *don't* steal other people's jokes. I sink down in my seat.

Next, Mrs. Adler asks each of us to say one important thing about ourselves, but I'm too busy fantasizing about throwing a pie in Ryan Rakefield's face to pay attention. I don't even notice Nick taking his turn, so I'm startled when everyone stares at me, waiting for me to talk. I accidentally blurt out, "I'm Louie Pie, and I like banana-cream burgers."

Everyone snickers.

Snickering is not the same as laughing.

"Is that part of your act?" Nick whispers to me.

I shake my head. Why didn't I say something funny? *Really* funny, I mean.

Ryan goes next and he says, "I'm Ryan Rakefield, and I'm the undisputed champion of the world."

More like the undisputed barf-head of fifth grade. I imagine giving Ryan an atomic-flagpole wedgie while the rest of the class take their turns.

When that's finished, Mrs. Adler hands out our

new books. The math book is huge and smells like the LMC. Then she passes something else out.

Something terrifying.

The flyer announcing the talent show.

FOR THE BARKER BACK-TO-SCHOOL BONANZA!*

DATE: Tuesday, September 29

TIME: 7 p.m.

PLACE: The Barker Elementary Gymnasium

COST: $5 per family

All proceeds go to the Barker PTA

**Attention fifth graders: We need your talent!*
Auditions for the Bonanza will take place
Tuesday, September 8, after school.

My heart starts to break-dance, and my armpits get damp. But don't tell my mom because then she'll start making me wear that deodorant she bought me.

I fold the flyer and stick it in my pocket. Dad doesn't need to see it. As much as I fantasize about doing the talent show, I don't have what it takes to do it in real life, and that's that.

Nick passes me a note. I bet it's about my act. Or about playing Turbo Toilet Tamers at recess.

You have to meet Thermos! the note says.

Thermos?

Who is Thermos? I write back.

Over by the flag. In the baseball cap. We met at sports camp.

Great. Sports camp.

If I hadn't been gone this summer in the Rolling Vomitorium (RV, get it?), Nick and I could have gone to Klown Kamp. Then he wouldn't have been playing football with Ryan Rakefield and hanging out with kids named after items in a lunch box.

I look over by the flag. A kid with medium-brown skin, wearing glasses and a backward Cubs hat, tilts back in his chair. Thermos. Never seen him before. He must be new. He's wearing a soccer jersey. Except for his glasses he looks sporty. I bet he's Ryan Rakefield part II.

We decorate our writing journals and write entries about what we didn't do over summer vacation. Then, the recess bell rings. The second we get outside Nick says, "Let's find Thermos."

I stop in my tracks and Ryan Rakefield bumps my left hip as he runs past me to the field. "Come on, Yamashita. Tell Invisible-Booger Boy you'll see him later," he shouts to Nick. "You can be my co-captain."

"Do you want to go?" I ask Nick.

He shakes his head. "Are you kidding?"

We both watch as Ryan divides the kids on the main field into teams.

"Look, there's Thermos!" Nick points.

I follow his finger to the edge of the football field. I bet Thermos wants to play football. Or kickball. Or baseball. Or soccer. There's a theme here, get it?

"Come on." Nick starts jogging, and in half a

second he's way ahead of me, like he can't wait to get to the field. Like he doesn't even remember that I'm his best friend or that we're heading right toward Ryan Rakefield.

I run to catch up.

"What should we do?" Nick asks.

"Mutant Eggplants Take Over the World?"

Nick grins. "Thermos changed it to Mutant *Soccer Balls* Take Over the World at sports camp."

Nick let Thermos change our game. My legs stop working and I stumble on a tuft of grass.

"Uh, I have to do something," I say. "I'll see you later."

"What?" Nick looks at me like I'm insane. But if I try to play football or soccer with Nick and Thermos, I might trip and get my legs twisted into a pretzel and sprain my kneecap and break my toenail. I can't risk it.

If Thermos had a basketball, things would be different. H-O-R-S-E is the only sporty game I play.

"What do you have to do?" Nick asks.

"Rearrange the pebbles by the bench?"

Nick folds his arms and taps his right foot.

"Okay, fine. Not pebbles. I am allergic to insulated food containers. What kind of name is Thermos anyway? Does he have a brother named Coffee Mug?"

Nick shakes his head. "Weren't you paying attention in class? If you were, you'd want to meet Thermos."

"I'll pass. Let's have a wood-chip war."

Nick takes a step backward. "Let's have one with Thermos." He takes another step back. "By the way, 'Thermos' is a nickname. Because of bringing soup for lunch every day. And Thermos isn't a he. She's a girl."

What?

I look past Nick to where Thermos is standing at the edge of the football field holding his—I mean *her*—own ball. If she really is a girl, she's keeping it a pretty good secret. She spins the football in her hands, takes a deep breath, then steps over to the huddle of boys dividing into teams and taps Ryan Rakefield on the shoulder. He says something to her and shakes his head. The other boys laugh. Thermos keeps standing there, but the boys ignore her.

"Are you coming?" Nick asks.

I shake my head. Nick runs off.

When Nick gets to the field, he and Thermos start talking, then look in my direction. I cross my eyes and stick my tongue out sideways. I don't

know why. Nick waves me over, but I shake my head and go sit on the bench by the doors and watch as Thermos and Nick play some game that looks like a cross between catch and the hokey-pokey.

I don't know what Nick is thinking. If Thermos is the kind of kid who wants to play football with Ryan Rakefield, she'll never want to hang out with me.

Sports

I can think of a million reasons sports are barfgusting!

First, they make you hot, smelly, and sweaty. Which means your mom will make you take a shower. If you don't play sports, then your parents might forget to make you bathe for three whole days. That actually happened one time!

Second, half the time your team loses. Or if you're me, your team always loses. Yeah, *that's* fun.

Third, you could break a leg or pop your eyeball out. The eyeball thing is real. But it doesn't only happen in sports. Some people can sneeze their eyeballs out.

ANOTHER REASON WHY SISTERS ARE WORSE THAN WEDGIES

At the end of school, the bell rings and we race to our lockers to get our backpacks. At Barker, only fifth graders get lockers. When I get there Thermos is standing at the locker next to mine. The lockers are in alphabetical order and her last name is Albertson. I must have missed that fact this morning.

She opens her locker door. The inside is decorated with pictures of famous athletes. At least, I assume they are famous. I don't recognize any of them. I'm sure Thermos wouldn't recognize any of the comedy legends hanging in my locker: Charlie Chaplin, Laurel and Hardy, the Marx Brothers.

"Hi," she says, glancing at me over her shoulder. "Is that Groucho Marx?"

"Yeah," I mumble. She must have heard me mention him.

"I'm Thermos," she says. "Nick told me all about you."

He forgot to tell me about you, I think. But I just say, "Oh."

Thermos grabs her football from the top shelf and her backpack from the hook. When she unzips her bag a green hair bow falls out and tumbles toward my feet. I reach down to pick it up for her, but Thermos dives for it and our heads smack.

"Ow!" I stand up and rub the place where my head bumped hers.

"Sorry." Thermos shoves the bow deep into her bag. Then she reaches out to my forehead. "You have a huge red circle there."

She has a matching circle.

"Louie Booger has a girlfriend!" I whip around and see Ryan, Jamal, and a bunch of the other football boys making kissy faces at Thermos and me.

I want to tell them to shut it, but that'll make things worse. I turn to Thermos. She's already halfway down the hall, like she couldn't wait to get away from me.

I grab my backpack. Then I step around Ryan and his henchmen to find Nick. He's at the other end of the hallway because his last name starts with *Y*.

Nick and I head out to the little kids' playground. Ruby and Henry wait by the curly slide. Henry is sitting at the foot of the slide and Ruby is trying to attach a pinecone to his forehead. I think it's supposed to be a unicorn horn.

"Do you want to hang out later? After I go to the eye doctor?" Nick asks. "Maybe we could invite Thermos, too."

"We could play Magical Mystery Unicorns Enter the Cave of Doom," Ruby says, repositioning the pinecone. "Louie and I invented it up this summer."

We reach the first corner and when we stop to look both ways Nick curls his upper lip in a classic *yuck* face. I can't believe Ruby told him that we played Magical Mystery Unicorns.

I shrug my shoulders. "What can I tell you? After ten days in the Rusty V. Hickle, unicorns start looking pretty good. Boredom makes you do crazy things."

Nick nods his head like he's remembering something. "Once, at sports camp, it was raining, and they made everyone play shuffleboard in the gym." Nick rolls his eyes. "Thermos and I made up a game called The Floor Is Hard. You fall down and say 'Ouch. The floor is hard.' It hurt."

"You should have played My Butt Is Soft. Then it wouldn't have hurt so much."

Nick laughs. "You should have been there."

At sports camp? With him and Thermos? Does Nick remember who he's talking to?

We reach the part of the sidewalk that is in front of my house and across the street from Nick's house. I want to say something hysterical, to remind him that comedy can be as fun as sports, but I can't think of anything. Ruby and Henry say goodbye and leave Nick and me standing alone. I should invite Nick to watch my act. You can't get a better audience than a best friend.

"Have a good time at the eye doctor," I tell him.

He bugs his eyes. "Call me if you want to hang out later."

After we say goodbye, I step into my house, hang up my backpack in the front hall closet, and edge my way into the kitchen. My dad is washing the dishes from breakfast. I wonder if he's going to make me do my act right away or if he'll give me a little while to prepare myself.

"Hi, Dad," I say, rocking back and forth on my feet. "I'm home."

"Hi, Louie," he says without turning around. "Did anything funny happen at school today?"

My dad asks me that every school day, but today his voice sounds hollow, as though he's asking because he has to, not because he wants to know the answer.

"Mrs. Adler accidentally told us to 'sit down in our *sheets*.' That was sort of funny."

I wait for my dad to answer, but he's scrubbing a frying pan.

"Dad?"

He keeps scrubbing and staring out the window.

"Dad!"

He starts and soapy water sloshes onto the counter. "Sorry, Louie. I was lost in thought for a minute there. So, did anything funny happen today?"

I check my dad's eyes for a twinkle, because he must be kidding. But there's nothing.

"Nah," I tell him. "It was the first day. Funny stuff doesn't start until day two."

Dad nods his head and goes back to scrubbing. He doesn't say anything about my act.

"Ahem." I clear my throat and my dad looks at me. "Are you forgetting something?"

His eyes are completely blank for a moment, then suddenly they fill with recognition. For some strange reason I actually feel relieved.

"Lunch," he says. "What do you want for a snack?"

A snack?

"Dad. Our pact? I'm supposed to do my act for you."

Now Dad's eyes fill with a different kind of recognition. "Oh, right. Sorry. Can we do that another time?"

I don't understand. Yesterday my dad couldn't wait to see my act. Today it doesn't matter.

A rubbery lump lodges itself in my chest. "Okay," I say, even though it doesn't feel okay. Maybe my dad decided I'm not worth pushing.

I take a deep breath. "When?"

"We'll see," he says. "My day was draining. Why don't you make yourself a Fluffernutter?"

"And then you'll watch my act after that?" Not that I want to do my act. But if I have to do it, I want to know when.

"Fine." My father sighs, and I start making my sandwich.

Fluffernutters are better than barftastic. They are barfmazing. The perfect sandwich: peanut butter and Marshmallow Fluff on white bread. My mom claims they are not "real food." Thankfully, my dad didn't get that memo.

While my dad finishes the dishes, I spread the peanut butter over the first slice of bread and figure out what other memos my dad didn't get.

"Can I eat this in front of the TV while I watch *Lou Lafferman's Laff Nite*?" Mom never lets us eat in front of the television. Another rule: no TV until after dinner.

"I guess so," my dad says.

"Can I have root beer?" No soft drinks unless we have company.

"Go ahead."

"Can I have a Lucky Charms sandwich?" Ruby waltzes into the kitchen. She's now wearing a ballerina tutu and my old Batman mask. "And can I watch TV with Louie?"

I roll my eyes. Whenever I watch TV with Ruby she asks a million questions and laughs at the wrong parts. But I'm pretty sure my dad will say no. A Lucky Charms sandwich is the messiest food on the planet: a kitchen-only food. I know my dad got the memo about that one.

He puts the pan he was scrubbing in the dish rack. "Fine," he says. "Try not to spill."

He might as well tell Ruby to take a bath but try not to get wet. I should talk my dad out of it. My mom won't be happy if she comes home to a magically delicious mess in the family room. But I don't. Something is weird about my dad.

"Come on," I say to Ruby, walking into the

family room. "Be careful with that sandwich, and if you talk during the show, I'll never play Magical Mystery Unicorns Enter the Cave of Doom with you again." Not that I was planning on it anyway. *Really.*

We carry our snacks to the coffee table and settle ourselves on the couch at the same time that Ariella and a horde of her friends march in front of the TV, blocking our view. For some reason every one of them is wearing jean shorts. And they all stand the same way—one knee bent, with their hands on their hips.

"Dad told us we could have the family room TV today," Ari says. "You have to watch in Mom and Dad's room."

"Dad said I could watch *Lou Lafferman*. It's not recorded on Mom and Dad's TV. Why don't *you* use Mom and Dad's room?"

"Yeah," says Ruby. "We want to watch *Lou*."

I take a bite of my Fluffernutter and try to click on the TV, but the giant group of girlzillas is still in the way.

"There's not enough room in there. You can watch your show later." Ari tries to grab the remote out of my hands. I yank it back and smack myself on the nose.

Ow.

The girlzillas giggle.

Ari and I squint into each other's eyes like we're about to have a gunfight in the Old West, then we both shout, *"Daa-aaad!"*

My father runs into the room with suds covering his hands. His eyes are wide and worried.

"What happened?" He looks frantically at everyone.

I don't know why, but that makes the girlzillas giggle *again*. What's the deal with girls and giggling? It must be contagious with them or something.

Ari smiles at Dad as sweetly as a rattlesnake. "You said we could have the TV in the family room."

I gulp my root beer. I'm sure my dad will remember that he told me I could watch *Lou*. But then he looks at me with his eyebrows pinched. "I'm sorry, Louie, but I told Ari she could have this TV."

"That's not fair. You told me I could watch *Lou*."

"I know it's not fair. Nobody ever said life was fair. I made a mistake, I'm sorry." Dad sighs and runs his soapy fingers through his hair, leaving a big pouf of bubbles on his forehead. "Be a sport, okay?"

You know what I hate more than sports? Being a sport.

"What am I supposed to do? You won't let me watch TV and you won't watch my act!"

"I'll watch your act," says Ruby.

Dad hangs his head. "You can have the TV as soon as Ari's friends go home." He slouches back to the kitchen.

"I love comedian shows." Ruby tugs my sleeve.

The girlzillas swarm the couch and suddenly I'm surrounded by them. It smells like I'm sitting in the middle of a strawberry-shampoo factory. Barf.

I head back to the kitchen. Ruby follows me.

"Want me to be your bannouncer?" she asks. "I can do a really good bannouncer voice." She makes a sound deep in her chest and starts talking low and slow. "Laaa-diesss and gennnntlemennnn . . . bannnnoun-sssing Louuuu-ie Burrr-ger!"

For some reason, I don't feel nervous when I think about doing my act for Ruby, but that's probably because she's a weirdo six-year-old who doesn't even know how to say the word *announcer*. It doesn't count if she thinks I'm funny.

My dad rinses his sudsy fingers, then stares hard at me while drying his hands on a dish towel. Maybe I have Marshmallow Fluff on my face. I wipe my cheek with the back of my hand.

"What?" I say.

My dad shakes his head. "I need to be in my studio for a while. Will you watch Ruby?"

His studio used to be Ari's room, but Mom made Ari move in with Ruby so Dad could have a space to create his masterpieces.

Suddenly, I remember something. "Your meeting! How'd it go? Is the gallery going to sell your art?"

My dad shrugs. "Guess your mom was right."

"Oh." I wish I could take my question back. "Sorry."

"It's okay, Daddy." Ruby hugs my dad's leg. "I'll buy your art."

My dad rubs Ruby's back. "No way. You get it for free." He turns to me. "Can I take a rain check on your act? I wouldn't be a good audience today."

My dad's words should make me feel great since I don't have to do my act anymore, but they don't.

He leaves Ruby and me standing alone in the kitchen.

"I will be the best audience in the world," Ruby says. "So will Sparkle and Magic Star."

"Sorry, Ruby. I wouldn't be a good comedian today. Want to play Magical Mystery Unicorns?"

Ruby's eyes widen and she nods. "Today is Louie the Unicorn's horn day celebration."

"Why are they called unicorns anyway?" I ask. "It's not like they have corn on the cob sticking out of their foreheads. They should be called uni-*horns*, right?"

Ruby laughs. "You're the funniest person in the world."

Too bad Ruby's the only person on the planet who thinks so.

Boring Stuff:

1. clothes
2. shoes
3. hats

(aka my audience)

Posters of my favorite comedians:

1. The Marx Brothers
2. Charlie Chaplin
3. Jim Carrey
4. Jimmy Fallon
5. Lou Lafferman

My stage, complete with silver curtain, microphone, a stool for resting my water bottle on, and the laugh-track machine I found at a joke shop near Grand Teton
LOU
THE UNICORN
Trapdoor to the dungeon (just kidding)
LOU
Hats
TO ARI & RUBY'S ROOM

NOT THE CLOSET!

A few hours later my mom brings home take-out. My dad was supposed to make dinner, but he didn't.

"We can't afford this every night," Mom reminds him, unpacking the plastic trays.

"I am trying to make money," Dad answers.

"That's not what I meant." My mother slumps back into a chair and lets her arm dangle.

My father brings five water glasses to the table and plunks them down. Ruby closes her eyes. I wish my parents would smile.

"What do you get when you cross California rolls with Bran Flakes?" I joke.

"I'm too exhausted to eat," Mom says.

"Did you get California rolls?" Ari asks as she walks into the kitchen.

No one acknowledges my joke.

"Pooshi!" I tell them. I make drummer hands and say, *"Ba-dum ching."*

"Pooshi!" Ruby cracks up. "I want pooshi. And unicorn rolls."

"I got California rolls, spicy tuna rolls, extra-spicy dragon rolls, and cucumber rolls for Louie." My mother stares at the ceiling as she answers us, as though she's too tired to lift her head. "I didn't even have students today," she says. "I can't believe how wiped I am."

Ari, Ruby, and I open our little plastic trays of sushi and start eating. My mom doesn't seem to notice that my dad is mumbling to himself as he grabs his pack of spicy tuna rolls. Finally my mother takes a deep breath and sits up. "Okay," she says, "let's hear about everyone's day."

"Ryan Rakefield is a footsniff," I say. "But Mrs. Adler's nice."

"Mr. Beauregard said I'm the most unique of first grade," Ruby says.

"That's a polite way of putting it," I add.

Ruby nods. "Mr. Beauregard is very polite. But Daddy didn't sell his art."

My mom puts her hand on top of my father's and squeezes.

Dad slowly unwraps the paper from his disposable wooden chopsticks, then he looks at my mother and smiles. It feels fake, but I'm still happy to see it.

My mother gives my father a kiss on his cheek. "It's just one gallery, not the end of the world."

Ari clears her throat. "Speaking of the end of the world . . . Did you know that I'm the only person in middle school who has to share a bedroom?" Ari pops a California roll into her mouth, and I wait for Mom to tell her that this discussion is closed, but instead my mother says, "I know giving up your room has been hard on you."

"It doesn't have to be hard on me." Ari finishes chewing and puts down her chopsticks. "This time I thought of a perfect solution!"

Ever since Mom and Dad told us about the Studio Plan, Ari's been trying to come up with alternatives. First, Ari said *I* should be the one to share a room with Ruby, but my parents said that I was too old for a boy-girl room. Then Ari said Dad should work in the basement, but my parents said it's too damp. Then Ari said he should work in the garage, but my mom didn't want him to be in a different building from Ruby while he works, and our garage isn't attached to our house. Besides, the garage is so messy no one wants to clean it out.

I think we're running out of alternatives.

Ari leans forward, her eyes twinkling. "My friend got her own bathroom by using part of the laundry room. They didn't have to make the house bigger. They moved a wall over and made the laundry room smaller."

Ari shoots me a snotty smile, and my stomach burbles.

"If we knock out part of Louie's closet and build a new wall in the middle of Ruby's room, then we can turn two bedrooms into three and everyone will be happy." Ari leans back in her chair, picks up her chopsticks, and pops another roll into her mouth.

"No way." I jump up from the table. "You cannot take away my closet. That's totally cruel and unusual."

"Calm down, Louie," says Mom. "No one said we were going to do anything."

I take a deep breath and pick at the seaweed wrapper of my cucumber roll.

"I will share my room with Louie," says Ruby.

I stare laser beams at both of my sisters.

"Ariella," says Mom, "we respect your need for privacy. Unfortunately, hiring someone to tear down walls and rebuild them would be expensive. We've already explained to you that our budget is going to be pretty tight for the next few years."

I breathe a sigh of relief, but then Dad clears his throat.

"Now wait a minute," he says, and he suddenly has a burst of energy. "We can't afford to hire someone to do this project, but I'm handy with a hammer. I could move the walls myself. I'll have the time. Galleries aren't exactly overwhelming me with orders."

Ari squeals and jumps into my dad's lap. "Thank you! Thank you! Thank you!"

My stomach jerks.

My mother shakes her head. "David, this is a big project. When will you work?"

"It's not fair to punish Ari when this whole artist thing might not even pan out."

"You have to be patient."

My dad runs his fingers through his hair. "I can do both. It won't take as much time as you think." He gives Ari another hug, then sends her back to her seat.

"But Dad," I splutter. "My closet . . . Where will I practice my comedy?"

"Yeah," says Ruby. "Where will you put Louie's stage?"

Dad's brow wrinkles. "I'm sure there's another place for it. What about the basement?"

"The basement is gross," I say. "You didn't want your studio down there."

"Okay, so we'll find somewhere else. How about a corner of the living room?"

"The living room!" My mother shakes her head. I do, too, because the living room is in the middle of the house, where everyone in the world would see me, would be able to *watch* me every time I tried to make a joke.

"I can't have my stage out in the open," I remind my dad. "It needs to be somewhere private."

"You could put Louie's stage in my room," Ruby says.

I don't even dignify that with an answer.

"I'm sorry, but I have to get something off my chest," Ari huffs at me. "You claim it's totally important for you to practice your comedy, but then you say it has to be someplace where no one can see you. Well those things are completely opposite! If you don't want anyone to see you, why even do comedy in the first place? It's so not fair that *I* don't get a room because you're a chicken!"

I open my mouth to say something back, something super mean, like she's such a witch that Dad should build her a cauldron in her closet so she can practice her evil cackle, but I only squeak in a tiny voice, "I am going to do my comedy in public someday."

"Yeah? When? When you're forty? By then you'll be way too old, just like Dad!"

As soon as the words are out of her mouth, Ari turns fire-engine red. Everyone looks at my dad and goes silent as a comedian with no jokes.

My mother puts both hands on the table. "You know what? This is too big an issue to decide in one night. I say we clear the table, go for a walk, and plan to talk about this again another time."

"That sounds like a good idea," Dad says, smiling. But the smile doesn't reach his eyes. I wonder if he wishes he could go back and change his mind about becoming an artist. Maybe he'd be happier if he had found another marketing job that he hated.

Following your dreams sounds like walking through a pasture of rainbows and flowers and unicorns, but it's more like trudging through a muddy field in the middle of a thunderstorm with no boots and no umbrella.

The Best Ways to Torture Your Sister

(A guide for brothers)

(I suppose these techniques could also be used by sisters who want to annoy their brothers, but I do not recommend this unless your brother is Ryan Rakefield.)

Copycat: Say whatever words she says and do whatever actions she does. She will try to trip you up by saying things like, "Louie loves unicorns" and, "I'm so happy I'm a girl," but you must be tough and imitate her anyway!

Almost touching: Move any part of your body—fingers, toes, and elbows work well—as close as you possibly can to your sister without actually touching her.

Hide-and-make-her-go-seek: Hide any object of hers; for example, Ari's new deodorant. Then sit back and watch while she tears the house apart trying to find it.

Compliments: Say something rude, but make it sound like a compliment. Then your parents can't get mad at you. When you see your sister in the morning, in your nicest voice, say, "Your hair looks nice. I like when it sticks out all over like that."

Staring: Simple, but barftastic. Stare at your sister and wait for her to freak out!

AS LOUIE'S CLOSET TURNS

After being forced to participate in the family walk, I race to my closet. Even though Mom said over and over again that nothing has been decided, that we are going to take a very long time to think about it, that we won't do anything if we can't come up with a good solution for my comedy stuff, I don't believe her. Ari won't give up until she gets her way, and when Ari gets her way, my closet is a goner. I should make the most of the time I have left. I stare at the sign I made for my door and run my fingers over the edge of it. How can my dad even consider the idea of knocking down my closet?

"Ladies and gentlemen and rubber chickens," I say to my audience, "welcome to the final episode of *As Louie's Closet Turns*, the heartwarming drama about a boy and the only storage space he'll ever love."

I get a few sniffles from my Pez dispenser collection.

"Previously on our show, Louie's evil sister Arismella hatched a sinister plot to take over Louie's Laff Shack, and she hypnotized Louie's entire family to go along with the plan. Tonight, however, a shocking secret is revealed."

My T-shirts gasp.

"Louie is . . ." I make the sound of dramatic *dunh, dunh, duuunnnnhhh* music. "Louie is *adopted*."

The T-shirts gasp again.

"That's right, folks. Louie isn't the child of David and Laurie Burger, or the brother of Arismella and Rutabaga, as originally thought. He is actually the missing child of the world's greatest comedian, Lou Lafferman, kidnapped at birth and hidden with an ordinary family by Lafferman's archenemy, Klappy the Klown, in an attempt to prevent the Laffermans from becoming an unstoppable comedy dynasty."

My jeans moan in horror.

"Don't worry," I tell them. "Young Louie has a plan. He will soon perform an act at the Bonanza nightclub, and once word of his amazing talent leaks out, his real father will finally find him."

"But what if he's too afraid to do his show?" a voice asks out of nowhere.

I search my closet. I know I pretend that inanimate objects are my audience, but I've never heard voices before. Then I notice that my closet door is ajar and a mini-unicorn is peeking inside.

"Ruby!" I shout.

"He's never performed

before." Ruby wiggles the unicorn as if he is the one speaking.

"He's performed lots of times." I yank the door open. "In his closet. Besides, it's none of your business." I point toward my bedroom door. She's not supposed to come into my room without permission.

"Rutabaga is adopted, too." Ruby's eyes are big and wide and serious. "She's Louie's *real* sister," she continues, "and she has a special bravery potion, and she can turn into a unicorn."

"Okay, fine," I say. Sometimes it's too much work to argue with Ruby. It doesn't matter anyway. It's only a stupid soap-opera spoof. I decide to forget about it.

"Want to play whoopee cushion hide-and-go-seek?" I ask. It's like regular hide-and-go-seek except you bring a whoopee cushion with you when you hide. Every few minutes you have to fill the cushion up and sit on it.

"Sure!" Ruby takes the whoopee cushion I hand her and races to hide in the front hall closet like she always does. I'll let her sit in there a few minutes before I pretend that I can't find her.

Next to the box that holds my whoopee cushion collection is the box that holds my rubber chicken collection and next to that is my fake barf collection. I have tons of comedy stuff in my closet. My stage isn't the only thing that will need to be relocated if Ari gets her way.

But if I can't perform in public, maybe there is no point in having a stage. If only Ruby's bravery potion was real. Or better yet, I wish there was such a thing as a talent potion. I could drink it and instantly become the best fifth-grade comic in the world. Then I wouldn't be scared anymore, and it wouldn't even matter if I had my closet.

Barftastic Games That I've Invented

(And how to play them)

1. Whoopee Cushion Hide-and-Go-Seek: I just explained this one to you. If you don't remember how to play it you need to get your memory checked.
2. Psycho Hamsters: Hamsters like to do three things: chew, run, and sniff. Psycho hamsters like to do these things at warp speed. So zoom around your house smelling and chewing everything.
3. Baby Bomb Squad: Position baby dolls all over the swing set: on the swings, trapeze, slide, rock wall, etc. Take a bucket of water balloons, throw them, and knock every doll off.

4. Magical Mystery Unicorns Enter the Cave of Doom: Get a couple of unicorns, turn off the lights, and let the battle begin. Unicorn horns are actually the deadliest weapons in the known universe.
5. Brain-Freeze Tag: Like regular tag, but when you get tagged, your brain turns into a solid block of ice and you must act like a zombie. Your brain can get unfrozen if someone sprinkles grass on your head.

WHAT'S THE DEAL WITH GYM?

The next morning, when I go outside to walk to school with Nick, I see that he's wearing glasses. At first I think they are fake, but then I remember he went to the eye doctor yesterday. I can't do anything but stare at him for a few seconds.

"Hello? Earth to Louie?" Nick waves his hand in front of my eyes.

"Sorry," I say. "You got glasses."

"Don't be sorry. They help me see better." Nick grins.

His glasses are made out of clear plastic and are almost invisible, but then, in a strange way, the fact that you can't see the glasses only makes them more noticeable. He looks different, and I feel like I stepped through a portal into a bizarro universe. I wonder if I look different to him, too, now that I'm not blurry.

"My dad might turn my closet into Ari's new bedroom," I tell him as we start walking to school with Ruby and Henry trailing behind us.

"No way! Where will you do your comedy?" he asks.

"Who knows," I say. Then I add something that isn't true, to see what Nick's reaction will be. "I might give up on comedy. You can't be a comedian if you don't tell your jokes out loud anyway."

Nick thinks about it for a long time. "I guess that's true."

I don't know what I wanted Nick to say, but from the heavy stone his words lodge in my chest, I know that wasn't it.

At school, after Principal Newton finishes reading the morning announcements, our class gets in line for gym.

Definitely not barftastic.

Our gym teacher, Mr. Lamb, is as large as a

refrigerator and made out of solid muscle. In a voice that sounds like a megaphone, he assigns everyone a number. We have to sit down in order on the red line. I'm number two because my last name starts with *B*. Thermos is number one.

Mr. Lamb tells everyone with an even number to look toward the clock wall and everyone with an odd number to look toward the drinking fountain wall. I turn my head, and there is Thermos. Up close I can see that she has two brown braids tucked into her baseball cap and a little birthmark next to her right eyebrow. She doesn't look at me. She's staring up at Mr. Lamb like he's passing out free candy. It should be illegal to be that happy in gym.

“The person you are looking at right now,” barks Mr. Lamb, “will be your gym partner for the rest of the year.”

I gulp.

If my life had a remote control, I would hit Rewind and erase that last part, because there’s no way I can be partners with Thermos for an entire year. Thermos is sporty, and I’m coordinationally challenged. Once she figures it out, she’ll probably tease me worse than Ryan Rakefield.

I almost raise my hand and tell Mr. Lamb that Thermos was staring at him when he said the stuff about partners, therefore technically Thermos is his partner. But Mr. Lamb is standing with his arms behind his back like a drill sergeant. The bigger the muscles, the smaller the funny bone. I keep my observation to myself.

Mr. Lamb barks, “Sit-ups. Odd numbers, hold your partner’s feet and count. You have one minute. When I blow my whistle, switch. On three. Hut! Two! Three!”

I wonder if my mom talks that way in gym class. It's hard to imagine.

Thermos grabs my ankles. It's completely barf-diculous that we have to be partners. If I get any mental trauma from this, I am suing Mr. Lamb. I put my hands behind my head and try to sit up. My stomach muscles start to shake.

"Come on, Louie!" Thermos cheers. "You can do it!"

I struggle all the way up and Thermos shouts, "One!" which means everyone in the class knows that I've only done one sit-up so far. Each time I make it to the top she shouts the number even louder. By the time Mr. Lamb blows the whistle again, everyone knows that I only did seventeen sit-ups.

"Thanks a lot," I say to her in my most sarcastic voice.

"What?" she says, eyes wide.

"Never mind." She's probably trying to get me to admit that I only did seventeen sit-ups out loud so she can laugh at me.

"Partners, switch!" shouts Mr. Lamb.

I don't want to hold Thermos's ankles. I am philosophically opposed to touching girls, especially with Ryan Rakefield fifteen feet away ready to make kissing faces at a moment's notice. When Mr. Lamb blows the whistle, I take my index fingers and place them on the big-toe parts of Thermos's gym shoes.

Thermos does her sit-ups so fast it's as if she has a motor. Her glasses bounce up and down on her nose. She doesn't even need me to hold her feet. Maybe she's not a girl after all; maybe she's a robot. The whistle blows again. Fifty-four. Thermos did fifty-four sit-ups.

"Okay, fifth graders, three laps around the gym." Mr. Lamb stares right at me. "No walking!"

Thermos races off and has already done a third of a lap before I've even tightened my shoelaces. You can't be too careful about shoelaces. If you don't tighten your laces, then you will probably step on a droopy aglet. That's the plastic part at the end. If you step on an aglet, then your shoe will become untied. Then you'll trip. Which will cause you to do a somersault fall. Then your eyelid will flip inside out and Ryan Rakefield will call you the Lidless Loser for the rest of the week.

Um, I take it back. That didn't actually happen. *Really.*

Thermos laps me and is way ahead of everyone in our gym class except for Ryan. He's right behind her. Thermos glances over her shoulder and speeds up. Ryan stays with her. Thermos takes the corner on the inside and Ryan falls back a bit, but then he gets a burst of speed and nearly catches Thermos again.

"Go, Ryan!" Jamal shouts.

Thermos and Ryan have half a lap left to go, and they are heading toward the finish line at a million miles per hour, but neither one of them is slowing down. I worry they are going to crash into the wall. It's a padded wall, but it still hurts when you crash into it. Please do not ask how I know this.

Then in a split second, Ryan spins around and ends his last lap by trotting backward. Thermos smashes into the wall, but Ryan acts like he doesn't notice and sits down on the red line without looking. It could have been a funny bit of physical comedy, if you forgot about Thermos. She sits down on the red line a few feet from Ryan, hugging her elbow and rubbing her knee. She brushes off Mr. Lamb when he asks her if she wants to go to the nurse's office.

Of course, by the time I start my last lap, I'm the only kid still running. Everyone in my class is sitting on the red line waiting for me to finish. They stare at me as I come down the home stretch, and Ryan calls out, "By the time *he* finishes, gym will be over!"

It makes my skin crawl. I wish I could teach Ryan a lesson. He doesn't know anything about real comedy. Real comedians can be funny without embarrassing other people. If I was in my closet, I'd do a hilarious finish to end my lap, like Ryan's, only a million times better.

Then my brain thinks, *Why not?* And before

I have time to provide the lengthy and well-documented answer, *Because that would be a huge mistake*, my feet stop running.

My plan is to fall forward, then do a last-minute somersault, like Gene Wilder did in *Willy Wonka & the Chocolate Factory*. If I do it perfectly, it will look barfmazing. Unfortunately, even though I tightened my shoelaces, I still manage to step on an aglet as I set up for my stunt. The second I start to fall I sense that my balance is off. My right foot has pinned my left. I tuck my head, hoping that'll get me rolling, but instead I land in a one-two forehead-belly splat on the floor.

Ladies and gentlemen . . . Louie Burger.

Everybody laughs. I laugh, too, like that was the joke I had planned. Hopefully, everyone will think I wiped out on purpose.

"Hey, Splatburger," Ryan calls, "I thought the only place you could belly flop was a swimming pool. Guess I was wrong!"

That sets off more laughter and sinks my little

HUFF
HUFF
HUFF
LOU
51
LOU
WHUMP!!!

ship of hope. Once again, instead of being a real comedian, I'm the class joke.

"Burger," Mr. Lamb growls, "tie your shoes."

I slink over to the empty spot next to Nick, forehead throbbing. He shakes his head at me.

"Did you do that on purpose?" he asks.

"That depends on your definition of *on purpose*," I answer, rubbing my forehead.

"Well, don't worry," he says. "I'm sure everyone will forget about it by lunchtime."

Maybe.

I'm not counting on it.

Confessions of a Fifth-Grade Splatburger

(Life's most embarrassing moments)

In first grade, I accidentally ate Louisa Planter's snowman eraser because I thought it was a Christmas cookie.

In second grade, I wore camouflage pants to school on field day because I thought they would make me invisible and that no one would see me hiding in the middle of the soccer field.

In third grade, when the entire school was sitting quietly in the hallway with our heads down for a tornado drill, I started singing "Bananaphone," because I forgot I wasn't alone.

In fourth grade, I wore a T-shirt to school that I'd pulled fresh out of the dryer. A pair of Ruby's unicorn underpants were static-clinged to my back for the entire day.

In fifth grade, I belly flopped on the gymnasium floor.

ANTIDISESTABLISHMENTARIANISM

On Friday before lunch recess, Mrs. Adler stands up in front of the class, clears her throat, and announces our first big assignment: the hero project.

"Each of you will choose one person, or maybe a group of people, whom you admire more than anyone else. They can be alive today or figures from the past."

As soon as she says it, fireworks shoot up my spine, because I know who my hero is going to be: Lou Lafferman.

"There will be three parts to this project: a biography, a letter, and an oral presentation."

Ryan raises his hand. "Are we allowed to work with partners?" he asks.

Mrs. Adler purses her lips. "Hmmm. A hero is a personal thing, but I suppose two students might have the same hero. Okay, I'll allow it, as long as the two students both truly look up to their chosen subject."

Barftastic! I look at Nick. We could do a Barf Brothers tribute to the world's greatest comedian!

Reasons Why Lou Lafferman Is the Greatest Hero in the History of Heroes

- He can make his face look like it got squashed flat. (Like when a guest says something crazy and Lou smacks himself in the face.)
- He always wears a tie with one of the fifty states on it because he's very patriotic.
- He has four toes on his left foot. He lost one toe in a freak knitting accident.
- His hobbies are skydiving, bungee jumping, and bagpiping.
- He has a pet shoe.
- He can flip his nostrils inside out.

This hero assignment is the best assignment in the history of assignments. I can't believe I'm going to write a letter to Lou Lafferman. I can't believe I haven't already written one.

When Lou finds out what a big fan I am, he'll probably write me back. He might even want to become my friend, or invite me to be on his show, or to guest-host his show, or even to come live with him and be his apprentice and take over *Lou Lafferman's Laff Nite* and inherit all his money.

Okay, okay. It's possible that I'm getting carried away. I believe the expression that would fit here is: *Don't count your comedians before they hatch.*

When the bell rings for recess, Nick grabs my arm and says, "Today you have to play with Thermos and me."

He pushes me out the door and toward the basketball hoops before I can ask him to be partners for the hero project.

Thermos is already on the far side of the blacktop playing basketball with the boys. Well, she's trying to play basketball. She runs up and down the court, making some great blocks, but even though she's shouting, "I'm open! I'm open!" no one ever passes to her or acts like they notice she's there.

"Hey, Thermos," Nick shouts from the next hoop over.

"Nick!" Ryan calls. "Want to play? We're short one man!"

"Nah," Nick calls back. "I'm busy."

Thermos jogs away from the basketball game. No one says goodbye. She picks up a red-and-gray ball from the side of the court and walks over to us.

"Hi," she says to Nick, dribbling her ball a couple of times. "What's up?"

"Louie and I want to shoot baskets with you."

There's a long, awkward pause. Nick elbows me in the ribs. Ow.

"Right, Louie?" he says.

"Oh, yeah," I say. "Right."

"Sounds fun," Thermos answers. "But are you sure?" She eyes me uncertainly, obviously not convinced about the three of us playing together.

And I'm not convinced about playing basketball.

Blah-sketball.

I can shoot okay, but when I try to dribble and run with other people jumping in my face, eventually I wind up on my bottom with one leg tucked behind my ear. That's why Nick and I only play H-O-R-S-E.

"We're sure," says Nick.

"Great! Let's play Antidisestablishmentarianism," Thermos says.

I raise one eyebrow at her. "Anti-disser-whatsis?"

She laughs. "It's like H-O-R-S-E," she says, "only it lasts a lot longer because there are so many letters. *Antidisestablishmentarianism* is the longest word in the dictionary."

"You love H-O-R-S-E," Nick says to me.

Actually, I don't *love* H-O-R-S-E. And actually, *antidisestablishmentarianism* is not the longest word in the dictionary. The longest word is unpronounceable. And the second-longest word, *pneumonoultramicroscopicsilicovolcanokoniosis*, is still longer than Thermos's word.

But Antidisestablishmentarianism doesn't sound that bad. "All right. I'll play it but I won't say it."

Thermos laughs. I don't. Maybe Thermos thought of a good game. That doesn't mean that I'm going to like her. You can't be too careful with girls. I speak from experience. Sometimes one of them (Ari) will finally be nice and play a game of Monopoly after dinner. The game will get intense, but you'll be winning since you have Boardwalk *and* Park Place. Then she will get a text from some barfnoying boy in seventh grade and her thumbs will be busy for hours. When she's finally finished, you'll hand her the dice, but she'll yawn and say she's going to watch TV because Monopoly is *so* elementary school. You know she's only saying that because you were going to win, but it still makes you feel like you forgot the punch line to your best joke.

"Hey, Louie," Thermos says after she makes a shot from the three-point line, "who are you going to choose for your hero project?"

"Lou Lafferman," I say, as I try to match her

shot, but end up short by about a foot. "How about you?"

"Kenji Okada," she says. "He's my favorite baseball player. He plays for the Milwaukee Brewers. That's where I used to live."

"Kenji Okada!" Nick says. "My grandpa loves Kenji. I was thinking of him, too!" Nick looks at me with my jaw hanging down and adds, "Or Lou Lafferman."

Nick tries Thermos's shot and sinks it, and I feel more alone than when I had no friends in my class.

When the bell rings at the end of recess, Thermos is A-N-T, Nick is A-N-T-I, and I'm A-N-T-I-D-I-S-E-S, so I pretend that I'm a character named Auntie Disses.

"Okay, kiddies, Auntie Disses says it's time to get back to work." I use a creaky old lady voice and hunch my back over like I'm walking with a cane. "No fooling around in class now."

"You do a great old-lady voice, Louie," Thermos says. "You're way funnier than some other people."

Her eyes dart to the basketball court behind us, where Ryan Rakefield is taking one last free throw.

"Louie's got a whole comedy routine," Nick says. "But it's not done yet."

"Besides, nobody will want to hear it," I say.

"I will," Thermos says.

"Yeah, but nobody else will." Especially not Ryan Rakefield.

"You won't know unless you try," Thermos says.

Too bad, I think, because I don't want to try unless I know.

Walking home from school, I'm still thinking of Thermos's comment, and I realize I also won't know if Nick wants to be partners for the hero project unless I ask him.

"Lou Lafferman is the best hero in the world," I say. "I can't believe I actually get to do a report on him."

Nick shifts his backpack and squints one eye at me. "Yeah," he says.

"So, do you want to be partners?"

"Um. I'm not sure who my hero is yet."

After that, I don't say anything.
And Nick doesn't say anything either.

When I get home my father is in his studio with the door closed. I poke my head in to say hello. He's reading a book with a picture of tools on the cover, and he asks me if I can make my own snack and a snack for Ruby, too. I say yes since that means I can choose any snack I want. Mom always makes me have fruit.

After I finish making a plate of pickles for Ruby and a Marshmallow Fluff sundae for me, I head to the computer desk in the family room to start my Lou Lafferman research. Just because Nick hasn't decided on a hero doesn't mean *I* can't get started.

Unfortunately, I was the only student who didn't find a book about his hero at school today. I'll have to research Lou on the Internet until I can get to the public library. I've already read through Lou's official Web site twenty-two quadrillion times. I could probably write his whole biography from memory, but there might be something out there I haven't found yet. I stick two pencils up my nose, eraser side, not pointy side, and get to work.

At first, I'm a little worried that I won't learn anything new. But then, guess what? I find a Web site I've never seen before, and I *do* learn something new.

And I quote:

Lou got his big break after he sent David Letterman a video of his stand-up routine every single day for an entire year.

My brain starts to sizzle. I might have the best idea in the history of ever. I take the pencils out of my nose and rise from my chair. My knees wobble as I walk out of the family room, down the hallway, through my room, into my closet, and look up at my poster of Lou.

I could video my act and send it to him.

I look up at Lou and gulp. "Should I do it? What if I bomb?" I ask. "How do you tell your jokes in front of people when you have no idea whether they will laugh or cry or boo and call you a splat-burger?"

The poster doesn't move, but I hear Lou's voice in my mind: *Bomb so big you take out half the town.*

Okay, then. Big break, here I come.

The Real Longest Word Ever

It has 1,913 letters. Anyone who can say it ten times fast wins a free puppy.

methionylglutaminylarginyltyrosylglutamylserylleucylphe-
nylalanylalanylglutaminylleucyllysylglutamylarginyllysyl-
glutamylglycylalanylphenylalanylvalylprolylphenylalanyl-
valylthreonylleucylglycylaspartylprolylglycylisoleucylglu-
tamylglutaminylserylleucyllysylisloeucylaspartylthreonyl-
leucylisoleucylglutamylalanylglycylalanylaspartylalanyl-
leucylglutamylleucylglycylisoleucylprolylphenylalanylsery-
laspartylprolylleucylalanylaspartylglycylprolylthreonyli-
soleucylglutaminylasparaginylalanylthreonylleucylarginyl-
alanylphenylalanylalanylalanylglycylvalylthreonylprolylala-
nylglutaminylcysteinylphenylalanylglutamylmethionyl-
leucylalanylleucylisoleucylarginylglutaminyllysylhistidyl-
prolylthreonylisoleucylprolylisoleucylglycylleucylleucylme-
thionyltyrosylalanylasparaginylleucylvalylphenylal-

anylasparaginyllysylglycylisoleucylaspartylglutamylphe-
nylalanyltyrosylalanylglutaminylcysteinylglutamyllysyl-
valylglycylvalylaspartylserylvalylleucylvalylalanylaspartyl-
valylprolylvalylglutaminylglutamylserylalanylprolylphenyl-
alanylarginylglutaminylalanylalanylleucylarginylhistidylas-
paraginylvalylalanylprolylisoleucylphenylalanylisoleucyl-
cysteinylprolylprolylaspartylalanylaspartylaspartylaspartyl-
leucylleucylarginylglutaminylisoleucylalanylseryltyrosylgly-
cylarginylglycyltyrosylthreonyltyrosylleucylleucylserylargi-
nylalanylglycylvalylthreonylglycylalanylglutamylasparagi-
nylarginylalanylalanylleucylprolylleucylasparaginylhistidyl-
leucylvalylalanyllysylleucyllysylglutamyltyrosylasparaginyl-
alanylalanylprolylprolylleucylglutaminylglycylphenylalanyl-
glycylisoleucylserylalanylprolylaspartylglutaminylvalylly-
sylalanylalanylisoleucylaspartylalanylglycylalanylalanylgly-
cylalanylisoleucylserylglycylserylalanylisoleucylvalyllysyli-
soleucylisoleucylglutamylglutaminylhistidylasparaginyliso-
leucylglutamylprolylglutamyllysylmethionylleucylalanylala-
nylleucyllysylvalylphenylalanylvalylglutaminylprolylme-
thionyllysylalanylalanylthreonylarginylserine

WHY DADS ARE SOMETIMES WORSE THAN WEDGIES

Saturday night is male-bonding time. Usually my dad and I will watch a funny movie, a stand-up routine, or an old sitcom. That's how I learned about my favorite comedians. This week I'm thinking about something different though: my big break. I've got a surprise for Dad.

After dinner, it's my turn to load the dishwasher. My dad tells me he'll be waiting for me in his studio. I rinse the plates as fast as I can, put them in the washer, and change into my Lou T-shirt.

His studio door is closed, so I open it a crack and project my voice into the room. "Gentleman, desk, and sofa, introducing the funniest boy in the Burger family . . . Louie Burger!"

I expect applause, or at least a "Woo hoo!" but I hear nothing. I push the door wider. A soda-can picture frame sits, broken in half, in the trash can. My dad lies sprawled on the couch, fast asleep with a book covering his face: *Do It Yourself Remodeling.*

I don't believe it. My closet's a goner and my dad didn't even tell me. Forget male-bonding time. I head to my closet and step up on the stage. The imaginary spotlight warms my skin. Rows of

imaginary people stare up at me, waiting for me to make them laugh. I grab the mike and start talking.

"Parents should not be allowed to have more than one kid. It's completely inconsiderate. How would my parents feel if I brought home an extra father? 'Don't worry, Mom and Dad, I'll still love you, but having another dad around will be fun for all of us. He knows five hundred and thirty-seven different card games, he bought me my own TV, and he has a normal job. I think we should let him have your bedroom so he feels like he's part of the family. You can sleep on the couch.'"

The crowd roars and an electric hum fills my body. If a pretend audience can make me feel this good, performing in front of a live audience must feel unbarflievable.

Later that night, after I've tucked myself in, my dad comes into my room and sits on the side of my bed. He hangs his head.

"Sorry I fell asleep, Louie. Can we do a makeup male-bonding time tomorrow?"

I turn my head to the wall.

"I found another old comedian for us to watch, Buster Keaton. I think you're going to love him."

"I didn't even want to watch a movie," I say, looking at his reflection in the window. "I was going to do my act for you."

My dad rubs his forehead and a guilty look fills his eyes. Good.

"How about tomorrow? Will you give me another chance?"

I know I said I didn't want to do my act for him anymore, but I need the practice. Maybe if I'm good enough, my dad will throw away the remodeling book.

"High noon," I say.

"I'll be there," he answers.

The next morning I'm sitting at the kitchen table trying to swallow Mom's wheat germ-blueberry pancakes when the phone rings. Ari and Ruby both race for it, but Ruby is quicker. Her hand is already on the receiver when we hear my dad shouting from the other side of the house.

"I'll get it! Don't pick up! I'm expecting a call."

He's too late.

"Hello. This is Ruby. Who is your favorite unicorn?"

My mother grabs the phone away. "I'm sorry. Hello. You've reached the Burger residence. May I ask who's calling?"

Ruby sits back down in her seat. "You don't need to ask that. They tell you that anyway."

"Oh, hi, honey," my mom says. She hands me the phone. "It's Nick. Try not to talk too long, and don't ignore the call waiting. Another gallery might call this morning."

I take the phone and walk into the next room. "What's up?"

"Not much," he says. Then he's quiet.

I wonder why he called when he doesn't have anything to say. Finally he speaks.

"I like Lou Lafferman, but I talked about it with my dad and I decided that even though he's my favorite comedian, he's not my hero."

"Oh," I say.

"I really, really, really like Lou Lafferman," he adds. "But I want to do Kenji Okada for my hero project."

"Oh," I say again.

"Okay?" he asks me.

"Sure," I say, even though I feel as flat as a wheat-germ-blueberry pancake. "Um, I have to go. My dad's waiting for a phone call."

"All right," he says. "Come over later if you want to hang out."

I would, but I'm not sure who I'd be hanging out with. Nick doesn't seem the same anymore. I head back to the kitchen.

The phone rings again. Ruby answers. "Hello. Burger residence. Tell me who you are, please."

My mother tries to take the phone, but Ruby turns her body and purses her lips, like she's listening carefully to the person on the other end of the line. Then she lowers the phone and shouts at the top of her lungs, *"Daaadddyy!!! It's the people who want to buy your art!"*

"Ruby!" My mother grabs the phone, puts her

hand over the mouthpiece, and listens. When she hears my dad pick up, she puts the phone back in its charger. "Sweetie, next time go in the other room and tell Daddy he has a phone call. No screaming like a wild animal."

"Wild animals can't even talk, silly."

I'm still feeling flat, otherwise I would say, *Ari's a baboon and she can talk*. But all I can think about is how Nick chose Thermos to be his partner over me. Thermos.

Then my dad comes into the room, and he has a huge smile on his face, a real smile, one that shines from his eyes and spreads over his entire body.

"They want to see my stuff," he says.

My mother throws her arms around him and gives him a big kiss on the cheek. "Honey, that's wonderful! See? I told you."

"No." Dad shakes his head. "I mean, they want to see my stuff today. Right now. I need to pack everything up and go into the city."

"But, Mom," Ari says, "you were supposed to

take me shopping today." She gives my mom a look, like it's some top-secret shopping mission. It's not that secret; they are going to buy Ari a bra.

"We can do that when your dad gets home," my mother says. "The mall is open until six. Or maybe the Yamashitas can watch Ruby and Louie while we're gone."

"Thanks," my dad says, squeezing my mom's hand and kissing Ari, Ruby, and me on the forehead. "Wish me luck."

Only later, when his car is pulling out of the driveway, do I remember: high noon. My act. He forgot about me again.

Marketing Dad vs. Artist Dad

THE ROTTEN EGG

After Dad is gone Ari won't stop talking about her shopping trip, so Mom calls Mrs. Yamashita and as fast as you can say, "But Nick is turning into a sporty kid with a new best friend," she's sending Ruby and me across the street. Henry opens the door and says, "Nick is up in his room. Want to play restaurant?"

I think that last part is meant for Ruby, so I don't answer. I head up to Nick's bedroom instead. When I'm right outside the door I hear laughter, and my stomach clenches.

I open Nick's door and there they are, lying on the floor: Nick and Thermos. They are looking at Nick's *Nutso* magazine collection and cracking up, the way Nick and I used to do. They barely notice me walk into the room. You can take your pick of expressions for this one: *On the outside looking in. Third wheel. Left out in the rain.* There's a theme here. Get it? I'm the rotten egg.

Finally, Nick looks up and sees me. "Hi, Louie."

"Hey, guys," I say, trying to sound like I expected to see both of them.

"Louie, check this out," says Thermos, pointing to the magazine. "It's 'Harry Snotter,' the story of a kid with magical boogers."

"Funny," I say, but I can't bring myself to laugh. I want to go home, or to play with Ruby and Henry—anything other than hang out with the Kenji Okada Fan Club.

Thermos closes the magazine and returns it to Nick's bookshelf. Then they both look at me like I'm supposed to say something.

"What should we do?" I ask.

"I don't know," says Nick, standing up. "Thermos and I were going to work on our hero project, but I guess we'll do that another day. What do you want to do?"

"Louie should do his act," says Thermos.

Nick looks embarrassed. "Louie only does his comedy in private."

"You've never seen it?" she asks him.

"I don't perform in front of other people." The closest I've come is the time I performed for Ruby's Prance 'n' Nicker Unicorns. They kept whinnying before I got to the punch lines.

"No offense," Thermos says, "but that's kind of weird. I've never heard of a comedian who doesn't perform."

Thermos's words hit me directly in the gut. She's right. If I'm going to be a real comedian, I have to perform for people, never mind that my skin has taken on the consistency of room-temperature baloney and my earlobes have started sweating.

Nick looks like he swallowed something strange. "Let's hang out in my backyard," he says. I don't know if he's trying to help me, or help himself, but

Lou's voice is in my head again: *It's now or never, kid.*

"No," I say, my breath heaving in my chest. "Thermos is right."

I'm either going to be great, or I'll be so bad they'll both barf. *Fail spectacularly!*

I clear my throat. The floor bobs and sways.

"I'm going to start with . . ." A wave of fear sweeps over me and I have to begin again.

"I'm going to start with . . . uh . . ." My mind goes blank. I think I even hear crickets chirping.

"With . . . uh . . . with . . ."

Nothing. I can't remember a single bit from my entire act. Not a joke, not a song parody, not a gag.

There is nothing spectacular about forgetting your jokes.

The door to Nick's room bursts open and Ruby and Henry barge in.

"We're bored of restaurant," Henry announces.

"I have the best idea," Ruby says. "Want to do a unicorn fashion show?"

"Go away," Nick answers. "We need privacy."

"Yeah," Thermos echoes. "Louie's doing his act."

Ruby looks back and forth between Nick, Thermos, and me with her mouth hanging open. Then she sits down and pats the floor next to her. "Have your seat, Henry. Ladies and gentlemen . . . Louie Burger!"

I shake my head. "You won't get it," I say. "I don't want you interrupting the whole time."

"I won't binterrupt!" Ruby says. "You binterrupted yourself."

I know she will, but I don't want to argue with my sister while everyone watches.

"Fine. I'm going to start with 'The Burp Song,'" I say. "I wrote it to the tune of *The Addams Family* theme song. That's a movie from a long time ago, and a TV show from a long, long time ago."

I take a deep breath, because you need a lot of air to do the fake burps at the end of the song, and I start to sing, never once moving my eyes away from Ruby.

As I finish, my heart thuds so loudly in my chest I'm sure everyone can hear it, because there's no other sound in the room. But even with my heart racing, I feel like the king of the stage. I nailed my song! Ruby jumps up clapping, and Nick and Thermos start fake burping, and Henry says, "Will you teach me how to do that?"

My heart rate returns to normal. I just did part of my act out loud and I didn't burst into flames or shrivel like a raisin or get booed off the stage.

"That was funny." Nick almost sounds surprised.

"It was great," Thermos says. "You should audition for the talent show."

Ryan Rakefield's face fills my mind. Singing a silly song in Nick's bedroom is nowhere near the same thing as standing up in front of a crowd of people who think I'm a weirdo. "I don't know."

"Come on," Thermos says. "You'll be great. Nick and I will be there, too."

"You will?"

"Sure. We have to go to the audition anyway

since we're going to do a pitching demonstration together."

Thermos is standing in front of me, still talking, but time slows down and her words become stretched and distorted in my head.

Aaaa piiitchhhinggg demmmonnsstraationnn.

"You'll see," she continues, unaware of the blip in the space-time continuum. "Doing your act at the audition won't be any different from doing it today."

I nod my head at her, though I'm not sure why. Inside, all I can think is, *Yes it will.* Because before this moment, I only *thought* that Nick had a new best friend. Now I'm sure of it.

Make New Friends but Keep the Old

Ever hear that song about making new friends? It's supposed to be about being friends with your old friends even when you make new friends, but the truth is right there in plain English in the middle of the song: *One is silver and the other's gold.* Those two friends aren't equal. One comes in first place and the other is just a runner-up friend.

Here's what the lyrics of the song should be:

New friends stink,
Old friends are true.
Don't wreck friendship
By adding more to two.

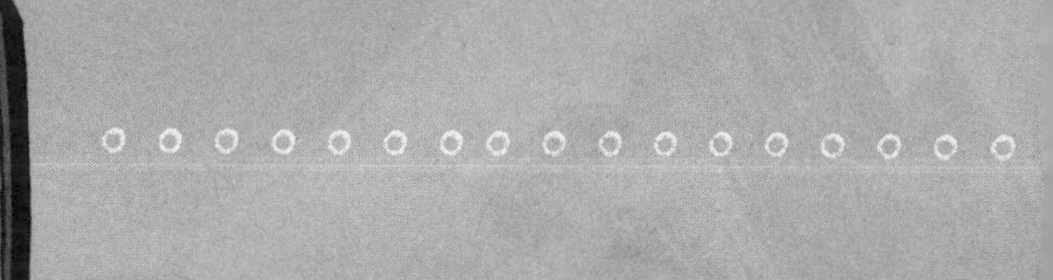

NEVER TRUST A GIRL

Tuesday afternoon before dismissal, Mrs. Adler makes an announcement.

"Auditions for the Back-to-School Bonanza are tomorrow. Don't worry if your act isn't complete. Anyone who auditions will make the show, but the other teachers and I need to approve your content. It will also be your chance to let us know if you will need a microphone or speakers."

The bell rings, and everyone runs for the door.

"I hope all of you will consider participating," Mrs. Adler calls after us.

I race to my locker, but of course I don't get there before Thermos. She's already shoving books into her backpack when I step up behind her. As she slams the door, I glimpse a pile of hair bows shoved in the bottom corner. I open my locker while Thermos steps back.

"Make way for the best act in the talent show," Ryan shouts as he and Jamal walk down the hallway.

"I'm sure your act is better than theirs," Thermos says as they pass us. Why is her voice always so loud?

"No way!" Ryan pushes Thermos aside and leans down to me. "*You're* going to be in the show?" he asks me. "What's your talent? Annoying the audience?"

What's yours? I want to say, *Making fun of the audience?* But my vocal cords are paralyzed. Then Thermos answers for me. "Louie's a stand-up comedian."

Ryan's backpack slides to the floor and he has to hold his sides from laughter. "Good one," he says to Thermos. "You sure you're not the comedian?"

Jamal laughs.

I want to shove cream pies in both their faces or spray their pants with seltzer water or at least tell them to go barf up a tree, but I can't, because their laughter has me frozen. This is what will happen if I do my act. Ryan will start heckling me. And then the audience will join in.

"He's good," Thermos tells Ryan. "Way better than you."

"Oh yeah?" Ryan's face gets serious. He hikes his backpack high on his shoulders. "I'm doing comedy, too. Jamal and I are going to do Abbott and Costello's *Who's on First!*"

Real comedy. Ari was right.

"Louie doesn't need to copy someone else's jokes," Thermos says. "He's got his own."

Ryan looks me up and down like I'm a giant bag of barf. "We'll find out tomorrow," he says. "At the audition."

My knees buckle. I need to get out of the hallway as quickly as possible, and I'm not coming back to school until the Bonanza is over. Thermos is insane.

I fling my backpack over my shoulder. Unfortunately, it is so heavy it spins me in a circle, and I bump my elbow on my locker door. Ow.

Ryan laughs. "Nice move, Geekburger." He walks away before I can think of a comeback.

"Are you okay?" Thermos asks me when Ryan is out of earshot. "You look kind of green."

I feel kind of unconscious. "Why did you say that stuff?"

"What stuff?" she asks, confused.

"That stuff to Ryan!" My voice squeaks and

several people in the hallway turn and stare. "About me and my act."

Nick bounds over. "What about you and your act?"

"It's trash talk," Thermos says. "Don't worry about it."

"What's trash talk?" Nick asks.

"Thermos ruined my life," I say, and I leave school alone.

"Louie!" Ruby calls after me as I burst through the doors to the playground and storm past the curly slide. "Wait!"

I keep walking, but she catches up with me. "Why aren't we walking with Nick and Henry?" she asks.

"Because I need to think," I tell her.

"About what?"

"About auditioning for the talent show. Now shhh." I bite on a knuckle and go back to my thoughts, while Ruby matches her steps to mine, and for once in her life actually does what I ask.

Okay, just because Thermos told Ryan about my act doesn't mean I have to audition. I could pretend Thermos is insane, that she made the whole thing up. I could hide in the bathroom and never come out. Or I could tell the truth: Thermos said I was auditioning, but she was wrong.

There's one problem. If I don't do my act, Ryan will tease me about it for the rest of my life. Of course, he'll tease me for the rest of my life either way. But his teasing me about being too chicken to perform will be worse than anything he ever teased me about before because it'll be true. The only way to shut him up is to do my act.

"Are you still thinking about auditioning?" Ruby whispers as we turn onto our block.

"Yes," I say. "Maybe. I'm not sure."

"Because, if you want, I will let you have my lucky unicorn. His name is Louie."

"Thanks, Ruby, but unicorns aren't lucky. They are extinct."

"Okay," says Ruby, but her tone of voice means

that I'm making a huge mistake. "You can change your mind tomorrow. Unicorns are very powerful."

I know I need something to help me through my act, but there is no way a sparkly purple horse with a pink horn on top of its head is the key to my success. No way.

THE AUDITION

When I wake up the next morning I realize that unicorns may be the sappiest toys on the planet, but, if there is a chance that they can help me with my act, they are my new favorite thing. While Ruby is brushing her teeth, I sneak into her room and find the tiniest unicorn in her collection. Its body is smaller than a quarter, though its horn is much bigger than you'd think. I shove it into my back pocket and sneak away. Ruby would have lent it to me if I'd asked, but I don't want anyone to know that I have it, and Ruby can't keep a secret.

For the whole day, every time I sit down, I feel like I'm getting a measles shot in my butt. It doesn't make me feel any braver, and when the final bell rings at the end of the day, I take the unicorn out and shove it in my desk.

Auditions are in the gym immediately after school, but I'm so nervous, I hide in the bathroom for ten minutes. When I finally get there, the auditioning fifth graders are waiting on the floor.

Nick and Thermos wave me over. Thermos is wearing catcher's gear, the mask resting on top of her head.

"You ready?" she asks me when I sit down.

I'm ready to run through the hallways screaming, but I don't say that.

Nick makes a sympathetic face. "Sing your song like you did in my room. Piece of cake."

More than half the fifth grade is auditioning. Mrs. Adler takes the stage and tells us to be quiet.

"There are so many of you, we've split you into audition groups based on your act. Musical groups will go with Mrs. Hotchkiss. Dancing, gymnastics, and other sports go with Mr. Lamb. And all other acts will be with me."

My left foot starts to shake. Groups wasn't part of the plan.

Thermos and Nick stand up and follow Mr. Lamb to the back of the gym. I'm on my own.

My pulse pounds in my temples and I look around to see who I have to audition with. A group doing a Monty Python skit, two magicians, a juggler, some mimes, a boy who spins plates, and Ryan and Jamal.

Mrs. Adler calls us up one group at a time. We have to describe our act and perform one minute of it. In the real show we will perform for three minutes. The Monty Python kids go first. I don't pay attention. I already know the skit, and I need to concentrate on breathing. Today, I have two goals: stay alive and do my act.

After the Monty Python kids finish, Owen the plate spinner goes. He breaks five plates, and

Mrs. Adler tells us not to move until JoAnne, the custodian, has swept up the shards. Then she tells Owen to practice more.

"Louie Burger, you're next," Mrs. Adler announces after JoAnne leaves.

I stand up, and my shaky left foot sends wiggles through my legs and into my voice box. I'm going to sound like I'm sitting on a washing machine.

I gulp as Ryan elbows Jamal.

"This song is called 'The Burp Song,'" I whisper. When I try to sing, nothing comes out.

At first no one says anything, but I can sense everyone wondering what's going on. Ryan has his hand over his mouth, like he's trying not to laugh.

"Louie," Mrs. Adler says, "would you rather tell us about your act?"

I would, but I can't take my eyes away from Ryan. He leans over to Jamal and says, "Thermos was right. He is hysterical."

"Louie?" Mrs. Adler says again. "Are you okay?"

The gym is so quiet you could hear a feather drop . . . in Antarctica. Both of the other groups have stopped their auditions and are watching me, too.

Then, from the other side of the room, I hear my song.

"I drink a can of soda . . ."

It's Thermos.

"I drink a can of soda . . ." she sings again.

I close my eyes. I remember the words now, but my voice box is hammered shut. Thermos sings the whole song:

I drink a can of soda
And make a sound like Yoda.
My stomach might explode-a.
I really have to burp.

She even does the burps at the end. People laugh.

Mrs. Adler says, "Louie, would you stay after the auditions are over? I'd like to talk to you."

I nod my head even though it feels like my scalp has caught fire. Actually, if my head was on fire, at least I could say I failed spectacularly. I was just the most unfunny comedian in the history of comedians.

Ryan and Jamal press their lips together like they are struggling not to burst out laughing. I can't be in the gym for another second. I grab my bag and head for the hallway.

"Louie!" I hear Mrs. Adler shout, but I don't

turn around. When I get to the hallway, I slump down against a wall.

"Louie?" Mrs. Adler pokes her head out of the gym, and when she sees where I'm sitting, she comes over and sits next to me. "You should be proud of yourself for trying out today."

"I couldn't do it."

"You have stage fright," she says simply. "Lots of performers do. My brother is a musician and he has terrible stage fright."

"That's impossible. You can't be a performer if you can't perform."

Mrs. Adler laughs. "No, you're right, you can't. But you can figure out a way to get past your stage fright. It might not go away completely, but you'll be able to work through it. My brother does a routine before each gig to get in the right mind-set: he shakes his head, shakes his hands, then shakes his feet. That reminds his body he's about to perform. He tells himself that performing isn't about talent, it's about giving the audience a present of music. Finally, he focuses on one person in the audience. Usually by the third song his stage fright is gone."

I look at my feet and squeak my shoes against the floor. "Comedy is probably different from music."

"You might be right," she answers. "But his tips helped me when I first started teaching and felt nervous about getting up in front of my class."

I don't know what to say. Maybe the tips work for music and teaching because the audience listens quietly for both of those things. Making people laugh is different.

"Well," she says, standing up, "if all else fails, you could try imagining the audience in their underclothes."

"Underwear."

"I beg your pardon?"

"You should say underwear instead of underclothes. It's funnier."

Mrs. Adler laughs. "I'll keep that in mind." She looks over her shoulder at the gym. "I need to get back to the auditions. Do you want to come with me?"

I shake my head.

"Okay," she says. "I understand. But promise me you'll think about what I said. You can do this. It might not go perfectly at first, but every time you try, it will get better."

I nod, because that's what she's expecting, but inside I'm shaking my head. I can only see my stage fright getting worse, because now bombing isn't an imaginary thing, it's a *real* thing. And it could happen again.

"Great," she says, then she goes back into the gym. I stand up and start walking home. When I get there I plan to take the posters down from the walls of my closet and tell my dad to start the demolition. It's safer not to be a comedian.

When I reach my street my mom's car is out front. Both my parents park in the driveway because our garage is so crowded with junk. I wonder why she's home early. At first I think it must be because of what happened at my audition, but then I realize that even if Mrs. Adler had called her right away, Mom couldn't have gotten home that fast.

"Hi, Louie," my mom says when I walk into the kitchen. She puts a plate of apple and banana slices in front of me and says, "How'd the audition go?"

I make a whistling sound like a missile falling and then pop air out of my mouth like an explosion. "I bombed."

She rubs my back. "Well, luckily this was practice. You have plenty of time to tweak your act before the show."

I shake my head. "I'm not doing the show."

My mother looks at the ceiling. "I don't know what to do with you and your father today." She sounds tired as she says this.

I shove three banana rounds into my mouth at once. "What happened to Dad?" I mumble through banana mush.

My mother gets a funny look on her face. "He

heard from the gallery he met with this weekend. They said his aesthetic wasn't what they were looking for. I picked Ruby up for him so he could have some private time."

I scratch my head. "Dad and I both failed on the same day." I crunch into an apple slice. It's strange, but I feel better knowing my dad bombed at the same time I did.

My mother grabs my chin and turns my face toward her.

"Louie, neither of you failed," she says. "Your dad is going to keep trying, and if you want to be a comedian, then you should keep trying, too."

"You wouldn't say that if you knew what happened at school." I remember the picture frame I saw in Dad's garbage can. "And how do you know Dad's still trying? Maybe he says he's trying but he's actually spending his time reading home improvement manuals."

My mom doesn't say anything, but her eyes get sadder and sadder as she stares at my face. If only there was such a thing as a stand-up tragedian. I'd be a shoo-in.

My mother squeezes my hand and gets up from the table. She doesn't say anything, and I figure that means there isn't anything to say. I was right. If my dad can give up, then so can I.

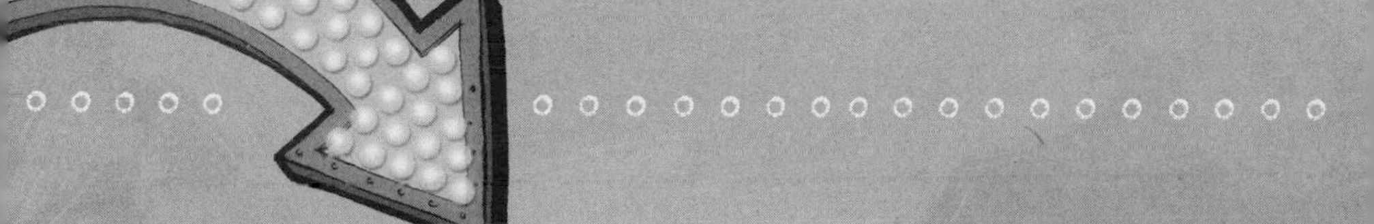

BAA, BAA, BARF SHEEP, THREE BAGS FULL

I spend the afternoon in my closet packing my comedy stuff into big black trash bags.

"Why'd the rubber chicken cross the road?" I ask my rubber chickens as I throw them away. I can't think of a punch line.

When there are three bulging bags standing next to the door of my closet, I sit down at the edge of my stage and put my head in my hands.

Ruby barges in, unties one of the bags, and starts poking around.

"Why are you smushing all your special things into the garbage?" she asks.

"I'm quitting comedy."

"Wow." Ruby sits down next to me and lays her

head against my shoulder. "I'd be humongously sad if I had to quit unicorns."

We sit quietly for a minute.

"Nope," she says. "I can't do it. I love unicorns too much."

"It's not the same. You don't have to do unicorns

in front of a million people. And even if you did you wouldn't care. You never care if people think you're a weirdo."

Ruby blinks.

"Do you think I'm a weirdo?" she asks. Her chin quivers.

That's the problem with sisters. You are having a perfectly fine time feeling sorry for yourself, then suddenly you are feeling sorry for them instead.

"Well," I say, "I do think you're a weirdo, but in a good way. It makes you interesting."

Ruby lights up. "You're a weirdo, too. I think you're the weirdest person in the world."

"Thanks," I say. Her words actually make me feel a little bit better.

"Can I have your stuff?" Ruby points to the bags. "I have a unicorn who's a comedian."

I look at the trash bags and I look at Ruby. I'm not sure what I want to do anymore. I bombed my audition. That should be the end of the story. But maybe it's not.

"You can have one thing," I tell her. "I'm not sure what I'm going to do with the rest."

Ruby jumps up and rifles through the bags, tossing the items that don't interest her over her shoulder.

"Careful!" I say as my Laurel and Hardy double bobble head bangs me on the knee. I pick it up and think about Stan Laurel and Oliver Hardy, one of the great old-time comedy teams. A lightning bolt idea blasts me between the eyes:

Not all great comedians are solo acts.

I imagine myself stepping onto the stage with a partner, and the thought of being up there doesn't seem half as scary. Maybe *that's* the key to overcoming stage fright.

"Can I have your jar of fake mucus?" Ruby asks.

"Sure," I tell her, though I'm barely paying attention. My thoughts are racing.

Doing my act with a partner is the answer to my stage fright problem. I'm sure of it. But now I have a new problem: How do I get a partner?

I want to call Nick right away. The Barf Brothers could be a great team, but I don't know how to ask him to be my comedy partner now. He's already doing an act with Thermos, and students can't be in more than one act.

I don't want to ask Nick to cancel on Thermos, but what choice do I have? If Thermos hadn't made me do my act in Nick's room and then trash-talked Ryan in the hallway, I never would have auditioned and my dream would still be nice and safe. The way I see it, Thermos owes me.

SLAM-CRASH-SMUSH BALL

The problem with asking Nick to be my partner is that we aren't best friends anymore. Before I can ask him anything, I have to become his best friend again. When Nick and I were best friends before, it was because we liked the same things. When we stopped being best friends, it was because Nick had started to like sports. Maybe I have to become a sporty kid, or at least a *sportier* kid, to get our friendship back. If that's the kind of friend Nick wants, that's the kind of friend I'll be. To start with, I will have to look sporty.

Unfortunately, I don't have any team jerseys to wear. The only thing I own that's remotely sporty is the terry cloth headband I got for free at the first and only day of tennis lessons I ever attended. I accidentally hit the ball at my instructor's head twelve times and he called my mom to come get me and told her she should never bring me back to tennis again. Ever.

Um. That didn't actually happen. *Really.*

After I've dressed for school, I walk to the kitchen for breakfast. When Ruby sees me, she runs out of the room, then returns with a pair of orange tights tied around her head.

"Why are we wearing headbands today?" she asks, taking a bite of her toast.

"I was going to ask the same thing," Dad says as he hands me a plate of scrambled eggs. "By the way, Mom told me what happened at the audition. It's my fault, Louie. I should have made time to watch your act. I'm sorry."

I take a bite of eggs and think while I chew.

"It's not your fault," I finally say. I wanted him to watch me, but I don't think it would have changed anything. "Mom told me what happened, too. With the gallery. She said you are going to keep trying."

My dad coughs and mumbles something I don't hear while he shuffles over to the sink to scrub the frying pan.

When Ruby and I step outside to walk to school, Nick looks at both of us funny, but doesn't say anything.

"Is today ninja day?" Henry asks, pointing at our headbands.

Ruby shakes her head and her tights flap behind her. "It's because we're quitting comedy."

I immediately glance at Nick to see his reaction.

"Sorry," he says, shrugging. "Thermos shouldn't have made you audition before you were ready."

Yeah, I want to say, *she shouldn't have*. But I wonder if that's what a sporty kid would say. "Thank goodness we have gym today."

Nick laughs. "Good one. At least you still have your sense of humor."

○ ○ ○

After announcements, my class lines up for gym. To start, Mr. Lamb makes us do push-ups. I manage to do twelve, though Thermos says she'll count the time I got halfway up as number thirteen. We do jumping jacks and I do twenty-three, but I accidentally step on Thermos's toes six times. Then Mr. Lamb blows his whistle and announces that we are going to play slam-crash-smush ball. Mr. Lamb invented it. It's dodgeball times a billion. I groan.

Then I remember I'm a sporty kid now. I pump my fist in the air and shout, "Yeah!!!"

A bunch of kids laugh, and even Mr. Lamb gives me half a smile.

He blows his whistle again. My eardrums quiver. "Divide into teams. Even numbers on the blue line, odd numbers on the green line."

I jog over to the blue line and only trip once. Everyone on my team besides Nick stares me down, clearly not happy to have me as a teammate, but I go around high-fiving them and saying things like, "Let's crush 'em!" and "They're going down!" so they'll know I'm the new sporty Louie.

Mr. Lamb sets out eight huge fluffy gym mats, which don't feel very fluffy when you get slammed into them, believe me. And he gives everyone a supersmushy ball about the size of a kickball. In theory, the smush balls won't hurt even if someone whips one at you, but this hasn't been my experience so far.

The balls are for tagging people. You throw the ball and try to knock your human target onto a mat. The mats are prison. The team with the last person standing wins.

When the game gets going smush balls are flying left and right. I run around as fast as I can—it'll be harder for my classmates to hit a moving target. This means I don't throw any balls, but it's only my first day being sporty so I cut myself some slack. Before I know it, I'm the only person on my team left standing and Thermos is chasing me around the gym.

Everyone on my team is shouting for me to pick up a ball, but Thermos is behind me ready to whip her smush ball as soon as I stop moving.

"Burger," shouts Mr. Lamb. "Grab a ball!"

That's when I realize if I can somehow manage to slam Thermos out and win the game for my team, I will prove that I'm the new, improved sporty Louie. Nick and I will go back to normal.

There's no way I'm going to beat Thermos to the draw. I'll have to distract her if I have any hope of throwing her out.

"Hey, Thermos," I shout, running back and forth.

"You forgot to hide your hair bow!"

Thermos's eyes go wide with shock. She instantly lifts both hands to her head, dropping her ball to the floor. I grab the ball closest to me and lob it at her. It isn't a very hard throw and it barely grazes her elbow, but it does the job. She steps backward to avoid the ball and lands on a mat. My team wins. Everyone jumps up from the mats and pats me on the back. Even Ryan Rakefield, who wasn't even on my team, punches my bicep and says, "Nice one, Louie!"

I look at Nick, but he shakes his head at me and walks over to Thermos. Her back is to me, but I can tell she's staring at the floor.

Mr. Lamb barks that gym is over, and everyone lines up to go back to class. I stand behind Nick, but he won't turn around when I tap him on the shoulder. Ryan and Jamal are behind me, and they are talking so loud everyone can hear them.

"Don't you love hair bows?" Ryan says, making his voice high-pitched and girly.

"They're so pretty!" Jamal answers in his own girly voice.

Thermos's shoulders stiffen, and Nick whispers, "Ignore them."

Mr. Lamb is ignoring them. He's standing at the door to the gym, looking out the window to the hallway and waiting for Mrs. Adler to pick us up.

"I like to wear a red hair bow when I play basketball and a green one when I play soccer," Ryan says. "But I save my pink one for when I'm with my boyfriend."

Thermos whips around, gets right in Ryan's face, and shouts, *"Shut up!"*

That gets Mr. Lamb's attention. "Albertson.

Cool it." He gives Thermos the evil eye. "You, too, Rakefield," he says to Ryan.

Thermos faces front and folds her arms across her chest. I tap Nick on the shoulder again, and he turns around, looking annoyed. "What?" he snaps.

"Never mind," I mumble.

Nick turns back around as Mrs. Adler arrives and leads us to our classroom. My feet feel sluggish and I want to explain to Nick that I wasn't teasing. Not on purpose. I was trash-talking, like a sporty kid. Why can't he see that?

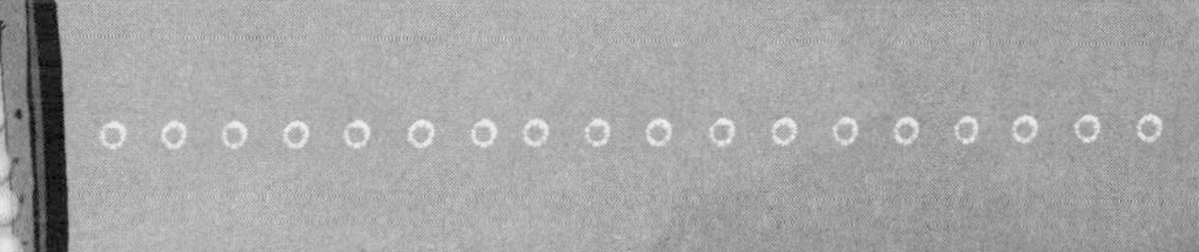

ALONE

I try to talk to Nick after school, but he speed walks the whole way home and it's hard to keep up with him. Ruby, Henry, and I practically have to jog.

"Would you slow down?" I say.

Nick slows down.

"Would you look at me?"

Nick looks at me.

"I didn't mean to embarrass Thermos," I tell him.

"Tell *her* that." Nick starts speed walking again.

"Wait!" I run after him. "I know you probably won't care, but I have a really big problem. That's the only reason I did it."

Nick stops. "I would care, Louie. That's the way

friendship works." His words are nice, but his voice is angry. He sighs and his next words come out nicer. "What's your problem?"

"I figured something out about my act. I need a partner to be able to do it."

"I'll be your partner!" Ruby steps in front of me, but I move her aside.

"Only fifth graders can be in the talent show."

"Oh," says Ruby, disappointed. She turns to Henry. "In fifth grade we will do a unicorn parade."

"Okay," says Henry.

I glance at Nick, smirking, but he won't look at me.

"I'm already doing an act with Thermos," he reminds me.

"I know that," I say. "Forget it."

Nick glares at me. "I don't get it. Why don't you like Thermos?"

Maybe I would have liked her if Nick hadn't made her his new best friend.

"She's the girl version of Ryan Rakefield," I say.

"You're so stupid. She's more like the girl version of you." Nick looks hard into my eyes. He storms off and Henry follows, leaving Ruby and me standing on the sidewalk alone.

When we get inside, the house is silent. My dad doesn't even shout a hello. I go to the kitchen and eat a snack, then wander around the house, bored out of my mind, trying to find something to do. I don't even feel like watching *Lou Lafferman*.

The door to my dad's studio is open, so I peek inside. Ruby is sitting on the floor making a picture on a giant geoboard Dad made for Ari when she was three. A geoboard is a huge piece of wood covered with nails hammered halfway in. You can stretch rubber bands around the nails and make designs.

My dad is sitting at his worktable with his eyes closed. He's so still, I'm not sure he knows that we are in the room. I want to shake him, but I'm afraid to move.

Ruby's creating a starburst design. I sit down next to her and add an overlapping zigzag border with blue, green, and white rubber bands. Ruby glances at me and then her eyes flick over to my dad, but I don't know what to tell her.

Ari walks by the door.

At first she goes straight past, but a second later she walks backward until she's standing in the middle of the doorway again. She looks at my father, then at Ruby and me. Then she walks into the room, sits down next to me, and starts weaving in little rubber band squiggles between the starburst and the border. She doesn't say anything either.

The quiet in the room is the kind of quiet that feels like it shouldn't be broken. Like library quiet. Or sunrise quiet. Or I'm-worried-something-is-wrong-with-my-dad quiet.

So we silently sit in Dad's studio stretching rubber bands, and before I know it, my mom's car door slams. We've been working for an hour, and my dad hasn't moved once.

Mom calls from the front hallway. "Where is everyone?"

Ruby, Ari, and I stop working, but don't say anything. I wonder if my dad will finally open his eyes. He doesn't.

When my mom finds us in the studio she walks over to my dad, puts her hand on his back, and says, "David?"

He finally opens his eyes.

"What's wrong?" Mom asks.

Dad sighs. "Everyone, I need you to gather around."

Ari, Ruby, and I stand near our parents so that our family forms a circle. "You guys have been so supportive of me, but I have made a decision. I'm not cut out to be an artist. Ari, you can have your room back. Louie, your closet is safe."

Ari bursts into a smile and hugs my dad, but my mom is shaking her head. "You have barely given it a try, and this has been your dream for as long as I've known you."

I search my dad's face. He has a million more wrinkles than he did yesterday. He smiles a sad smile. "Some things aren't meant to be."

I don't like that expression very much. I don't think my dad does either. He doesn't look happy or even relieved. He looks depressed.

What Mom said is right. Being an artist has always been Dad's dream. But maybe wanting to do something isn't enough to make it happen.

THE ULTIMATE BATTLE OF DOOM

For the next two weeks, whenever I see Nick I try to make a joke to break the icy force field between us, but it's not working. On the way to school, Nick walks five steps ahead of me, and no matter how fast I try to walk, I can never catch up to him. On the way home from school, it's the same thing. In school, Nick won't pass notes with me, and he sits next to Thermos at lunchtime.

On Saturday morning, three days before the talent show, I dream about Nick and me sharing a meat-lover's pizza. We both eat slice after slice, but the pizza box never empties. The best part of the dream is the way Nick and I laugh about it. Like we are Barf Brothers again. I wish it was true.

I have to tell him I don't care about the talent show, I just want to be friends again. I'm about to get out of bed and call him, even though my mom would probably say it's too early to call, when I hear moaning and groaning coming from my closet. Ruby must be in there playing Magical Mystery Unicorns Enter the Cave of Doom.

"Ruby!" I shout. "Who said you could play in my closet? I know it wasn't me because I don't talk in my sleep!"

Ruby cracks open the door and pokes her head out. "You can be Firespark."

"No way." I pull my pillow over my head.

"He's hiding from Blackthorn," she explains. "But the doom spies are on his tail."

"Ruby," I mumble through my pillow. "Go play in your own room."

"I can't," she says. "Ari is on the phone with Danny. She kicked me out."

I sit up. "Who's Danny?"

"A magic boy from seventh grade. And she needs to be private with him."

So, because Ari needs privacy, *I* have to wake up early on a Saturday. Thank goodness she'll have her own room back soon.

I slip into my bathrobe and slippers and tiptoe across the hall. I press my ear up against the door and hear giggling. With the way girls are always giggling, I don't see how they ever get boyfriends in the first place. One good thing about Thermos, she doesn't giggle.

I walk into my sisters' room and sit down on Ruby's bed. Through the window, I can see Mr. Yamashita mowing his front lawn. I have a good feeling about my phone call to Nick today. We've been friends forever, he's not going to forget about that. He might even be planning on calling me himself.

Ari shoots me a look of death. "Get out," she whispers, holding her cell phone away from her head.

I put my feet up on Ruby's bed, tuck my hands behind my head, and lay back on the pillow. "Why?" I ask. "So you can talk with your *boyfriend*?"

I should probably feel guilty about being the

world's most annoying younger brother, but that's the point. If I have to be pestered by Ruby, then Ari has to be pestered by me.

Ari stares me down like she's trying to melt off my skin. From the look in her eyes, I almost worry that it's going to work, but my skin feels as cool as ice cream with a dollop of Marshmallow Fluff. I made that expression up, by the way.

"Louie, I mean it. Get out." She throws her pillow at me, but it doesn't even hit the bed.

"I can't," I say. "My room's been invaded by Ruby."

Ari sighs. "Hold on," she says to Danny. Then she covers the phone and looks back at me. "Give me fifteen more minutes, I'll come get her when I'm done."

I'm about to complain when I see a car pull into Nick's driveway. Thermos gets out wearing a softball uniform. She rings Nick's doorbell, and Nick steps outside. Then he gets into Thermos's car, and the car drives away.

My eyes start blinking and I can't stop them. I guess Nick wasn't thinking about making up.

I remember my dad's words: *Some things aren't meant to be.*

I climb off Ruby's bed and trudge back to my closet. In the background, I hear Ari say to Danny, "*That* was weird."

Ruby has turned my entire closet into a unicorn hideout, but I don't complain anymore. It's not like I have anything else to do today. I pick up Firespark and Blackthorn and pretend they are battling for ultimate control of Unicornicopia.

Blackthorn jams his horn into Firespark's side, and Firespark falls off the edge of my desk—I mean, off the edge of the cliff.

"Help me," he calls to Magic Star. "I'm dying."

Ruby prances Magic Star over to Firespark and nuzzles his neck. I make Firespark flop around a little more, but my heart isn't in it.

Ari pokes her head in my closet and says, "I'll play with Ruby now."

"That's okay." I sigh.

Ari comes over and sits next to me. "Are you sure?"

I nod my head but don't talk. My throat feels sticky. I don't want to admit that I've lost my friend forever.

"Can I play?" Ari asks.

I pretend to faint, but Ruby holds up two unicorns. "You can be Nickleby and Thermostasia."

Ariella prances Thermostasia around and makes her voice really high-pitched. "I'm the most beautiful unicorn in the world."

"Thermostasia is a tough unicorn," whispers Ruby.

"Oh," says Ari, still keeping her voice high and squeaky. "I'm the toughest unicorn in the world."

"Better," says Ruby. She prances Louie the unicorn and Magic Sparkle over to Thermostasia and Nickleby. "Let's be a team. Then we can all defeat Blackthorn."

"Unicorn Power!" says Ari. She points Nickleby at Firespark, my injured unicorn. "We need you, too."

"I can't," I croak. "Blackthorn's horn is poisonous."

Ruby shakes Magic Sparkle over Firespark and glitter sprinkles down. "It's the antigoat. Now you can never get hurt again."

Ari giggles. I smile at her. Sometimes sisters aren't so bad. I stand Firespark up and prance him across my stage. My dumb old stage didn't help me become a comedian, but at least it's good for something.

Louie Burger's List of Made-up Idioms and Expressions

As cool as ice cream with a dollop of Marshmallow Fluff: Very relaxed and calm. When teasing your sisters it's important to act *as cool as ice cream with a dollop of Marshmallow Fluff.*

Marches to the beat of a baked potato: Very strange. We all know who *marches to the beat of a baked potato.*

Back like barf: Something unwanted that returns anyway. I had hoped he would move away over the summer, but Ryan Rakefield was *back like barf.*

Closet-sized: Hugely excellent. Doing my hero project on Lou Lafferman was a *closet-sized* idea.

THE BARFTASTROPHE

That night after dinner, I climb into the corner of the couch and pull a blanket over my head. I'm going to have to do the talent show alone. I'll probably fail, and not even spectacularly. But worse than that, I'm going to have to do the rest of fifth grade alone.

After a few minutes, I hear my dad's muffled footsteps on the carpet of the family room. "How about some frozen grapes?" he asks me.

I pull the blanket down and raise one eyebrow. Even though I'm feeling as low as a wart on the bottom of a Chihuahua's toe, I still would have preferred a less healthy snack.

Dad hands me a plate. "Ready for male-bonding time?"

"I'm not in the mood."

Dad pops a grape into his mouth and puts his plate down. Then he sits beside me, wraps his arm around my shoulder, and pulls me close. "Do you want to talk about it?"

I rub my forehead against his shirt. "I was going to ask Nick to be my comedy partner, but he doesn't even want to be my friend anymore," I say. "So now I'm going to bomb, and I have no friends."

My dad pats my knee. "You won't bomb. Not if you believe in yourself. And you and Nick will work it out. You've been best friends since you were babies."

"Some things aren't meant to be," I remind him.

My dad's eyes dim, and guilt swells inside me.

He runs his fingers through his hair. "Some things *are* meant to be. You'll figure something out. Great comedians always rise to the challenge."

I want to ask him why comedians are any different from artists, but instead I say, "Like who?"

"Well, take Buster Keaton," he says, holding up a DVD of a black-and-white movie called *Steamboat Bill, Jr.* "Legend has it that when Buster was only three years old, he cut the tip of his finger off in a clothes wringer, got hit in the head with a brick, and was carried two blocks by a tornado all in one day."

I wrinkle my eyebrows and look at my dad. "Seriously?" I thought *I* was prone to injury.

My dad nods. "He turned his troubles into comedy."

I don't think it will help my act, but if there is a comedian out there who's klutzier than me, I want to see it. As soon as the movie starts, my dad and I crack up. Buster Keaton is a comedy genius. The funniest part is when a wild storm blows a house down on top of Buster. He doesn't get hurt because he was standing in the exact spot where the open window landed.

When the movie is over, Dad walks me back to my room and tucks me in like when I was little.

"Buster Keaton was funny, smart, and clever,

like you." He kisses me on the forehead. "You'll figure out a way to solve your problem."

Dad lingers by the door for a second, then turns out the light. I pull my covers up to my chin because vampires don't come into your room at night if your neck isn't visible. Then I roll over, close my eyes, and hope my dad is right.

∘ ∘ ∘

When I wake up on Sunday morning, I still don't have a way to solve my problem, but I *know* I have to keep trying. Maybe my dad doesn't mind quitting, but it makes me feel like a deflated balloon. And not being friends with Nick makes me feel even worse. As soon as breakfast is over, I call his house.

"Hi, Mrs. Yamashita," I say when Nick's mother answers the phone. "May I please speak with Nick?"

"Sure, Louie, but Nick can't play today. Henry is sick and I want to keep Nick home for the next twenty-four hours, in case he comes down with the virus, too."

"That's okay," I say. "I just want to talk."

"All right," Mrs. Yamashita says. "I'll get him."

I stare out the window at Nick's house while I wait for him to pick up the phone, but a few seconds later when a voice says, "Louie?" it's not the voice I want to hear. It's still Mrs. Yamashita. "I'm sorry, honey. Nick says he's feeling too tired to talk. I hope he's not getting sick."

He's just sick of me. "Tell him I hope he feels better."

"I will," she answers. Then we hang up.

o o o

On Monday morning I feel so nervous about seeing Nick that my stomach flutters have flutters. I don't know if he'll walk to school with me. But when Ruby and I leave our house, there he is, standing at the end of my driveway. Henry must still be sick.

"Hey," I say, because I don't think you can do a packheader or a secret handshake when your friend is mad at you.

"I talked it over with Thermos. I'll do your act with you."

A huge bubble of excitement fills my body. He said yes! But then I realize how flat his voice sounded when he told me, how *un*excited he sounded, and the bubble deflates.

"Are you sure? You don't have to."

Nick sighs a sigh so loud I'm certain my dad can hear it in the house. "I wouldn't have agreed to do it if I wasn't sure."

My cheeks burn. Nick is doing what I wanted, but it feels terrible.

I should tell Nick to do the pitching demonstration with Thermos and that I will figure out some other way to do my act. But I don't. I'm too chicken.

Having a comedy partner doesn't feel the way I thought it would.

After the Pledge of Allegiance, we start our hero presentations. Mrs. Adler makes us put our note cards inside our desks so we won't be distracted during someone else's speech. Then she passes out bags of popcorn to munch on while we watch. Everyone settles in.

I think of a double-beat joke, and I want to whisper it to Nick, but I'm afraid of his reaction. For the first time ever, it feels safer to say it out loud to the class instead.

"After we eat this, do we have to take a pop-corn quiz?" (Get it? Pop quiz.)

The joke gets a few laughs and a few groans, but that's okay. I was setting up part two.

"Sorry. That was corny," I say. (Get it? Corn-y.) More people laugh the second time around. Mrs. Adler winks at me.

"No quiz," she says. "But I do expect you to gain a few *kernels* of knowledge."

I smile. Not too shabby, Mrs. Adler. Not too shabby.

Thermos and Nick go first. They set up a colorful poster with a baseball diamond. Each base is a different part of Kenji Okada's life. A little paper baseball player moves around the bases. When they put him on first base, they tell us all about how Kenji's father made him practice every day for two hours before school and two hours after school.

Whoa! Now that's being pushed by your father.

Then they tell us that when he first played in Japan, no teams wanted to sign him because he was too skinny. Who knew I had so much in common with Kenji Okada?

When Nick and Thermos finish, everyone claps, and Mrs. Adler tells them that their presentation was very creative. Next, Owen presents his report on James Dewar, the inventor of the Twinkie. Twinkies *are* an important contribution to society, but if I were Owen I would have chosen Archibald Query, the inventor of Marshmallow Fluff.

I can't pay attention. I'm too antsy about my turn.

Usually doing a report isn't as scary as doing stand-up comedy. I can read from my notes and stare at the floor and it doesn't matter if I'm terrible. But today when I step to the front of the classroom, my breathing starts to race and my mouth gets so dry my lips stick to my teeth.

I glance at Ryan Rakefield and my heart *ka-thunks* in my chest.

I glance at Nick. He has a faraway look in his eyes.

"Okay, Louie, go ahead." Mrs. Adler smiles encouragingly from the side of the room.

My hands shake, but I look down at my note cards and begin.

"Lou Lafferman was born on March 8, 1980. He told his first joke at age three. 'Why did the chicken cross the road? Elbow!' As you can see, he wasn't very good when he started, but he kept working at it."

I try to catch Nick's eye. I wish he would give me some sign that we can be friends again. He has a sour expression on his face. Does he wish he could leave? Does he hate my speech? I lose track of my words and stare at Nick. A couple of kids clear their throats, and Mrs. Adler says, "Louie? Remember the tips?"

I don't answer because Nick looks really strange. I tilt my head and wonder how a person's skin can get that shade of green.

Mrs. Adler notices, too. "Nick, are you all right?"

Nick nods and then hurls onto his desk.

Only one kid says, "Eeew" out loud, but I'm sure

everyone is thinking it. It's obvious Nick had Froot Loops for breakfast, although they've lost their lemony-grapy smell. Even from the front of the room, I can tell.

Mrs. Adler runs to the sink, grabs two fistfuls of paper towels, then rushes over to Nick. She helps him wipe his mouth and spreads the rest of the towels on top of the puke. Then she tells Thermos to walk Nick to the nurse with his coat and backpack. After they leave, she calls JoAnne to come to our room for a cleanup.

I'm still standing at the front of the room, holding my report so tightly the cards crumple. Poor Nick. I hope he feels better soon.

But something dawns on me, and I almost feel like *I* have to barf. Nick can't do the talent show now. Barf Brothers can't perform when they're barfing for real. Even if he feels better tomorrow, there is no way his mom will let him out of the house so soon. I'm right back where I started. Alone, and about to humiliate myself in front of the entire school.

Top Five Most Boring Jobs I Might Have to Do if I Can't Cut It as a Comedian

1. Toilet-Bowl Scrubber (The person, not the scrub brush.)
2. Insurance Analyst (I don't even know what that is.)
3. Lined-Paper Salesman (You should buy this really exciting product . . . paper! Nope. I don't think so.)
4. Banker (If you have to wear a suit and tie, how much fun can you have?)
5. Gym Teacher (Doesn't even need an explanation.)

THE BARF SISTER

At recess, kids are fake barfing everywhere I look. The weather is especially sunny and warm for the end of September, but that only makes me feel worse. It should be cold and rainy. That would fit my mood better. I hide in the shady spot behind the rock-climbing wall, but Thermos finds me. My gut tightens. Is she going to yell at me for what I said in gym? Is she going to yell at me for asking Nick to be my partner?

Is she going to beat me up?

She's got a piece of paper in her hands and she shoves it toward me. "Nick asked me to give you this. He wrote it in the nurse's office."

"Thanks," I say, but I don't open it. What if it says:

Ha! You got what you deserve. Now you'll never be a comedian.

Thermos leaves without saying anything else and trudges to the edge of the football game to watch. Without Nick, she's as alone as I am.

Now that she's gone, I look at Nick's note. On the outside is written:

For Louie's eyes only.

My hands shake as I unfold the paper. The future of our friendship is inside. Hopefully it will say something like:

No matter how sick I am, I won't miss the talent show. You're my best friend.

What it actually says is:

Thermos could be your partner.

Nick wants me to do my act with *Thermos.*

I imagine stepping out onto the stage with Thermos by my side and I don't feel the zingy buzz I get when I imagine performing with Nick. But I don't feel filled with fear and dread either.

It would probably be better than performing alone, but there is no way Thermos would agree to it.

I stand and take one step toward the football field.

This might be the dumbest thing I've ever done.

I take another few steps.

Thermos knows kung fu. She could turn me into tiny pieces of Louie.

A few more steps, and Thermos glances over her shoulder and sees me coming. I quickly squint up at the sky as if I have spotted a UFO. When I look back at Thermos, she's studying the skies too. I manage to jog the rest of the way before she notices me again. I don't want to give her time to run away from me.

The football boys act as if they don't see Thermos on the sidelines. They're probably scared of her, she's so much better at football than they are.

"They said they'd let me in if anyone got injured, but I don't believe them."

I shade my eyes. The sun is behind her head, so

it's hard to look at her face. I shift my gaze to the grass.

"You'd think sporty kids would be good at sportsmanship," I say.

Thermos looks me up and down. "Kids aren't like books. You can't tell from the outside what they're like on the inside."

"Also, we're more waterproof," I joke.

Thermos doesn't laugh.

"Sorry," I say. I made a huge mistake coming over here. "Bad joke. I just wanted to tell you what Nick's note said. If you want to know."

Thermos puts a hand on her hip and taps her foot. "Okay."

"He wanted me to ask you to be my partner for the talent show."

Thermos bends down, rips up a handful of grass, and sprinkles it on the ground.

"He was going to do it, but I guess you already know that. And since you can't do a pitching demonstration without . . . Well, I guess we both need a part—"

Thermos cuts me off.

"I switched to a dribbling demonstration."

"Oh." Right. She wouldn't drop out of the talent show just because Nick changed partners. Most people don't have a problem performing alone. "A dribbling demonstration sounds neat. You'll be great at it!"

I turn and run back to the shady spot by the rock-climbing wall before Thermos can say anything else. My heart is skittering and my whole body jitters with nerves. I only have two options left: either I have to kill, or I have to fail so spectacularly the audience won't know what hit them.

AND THEN THERE WAS BARF

The next evening, when it's time to leave for the talent show, my ears are ringing and my palms are so sweaty my rubber chicken slips right out of my grip. Mom announces that we all have to get in the car now or we're going to be late. I grab the giant cardboard Chicago skyline poster I made. It's my backup plan for failing. If nobody laughs, I will bring it out and do a Buster Keaton. The whole thing will fall and squash me flat.

Ari, Ruby, and I get in the car. Mom loads the skyline in the back and honks the horn for Dad. He rushes out carrying a suspicious small gray bag.

"Hey! I said no pictures or video!"

"Come on, Louie," my dad moans. "It's a big night. You might want to see it someday."

"Definitely not." I put my hand on the door handle. "I won't perform if you are going to record it."

Mom gives my dad a look. "Don't worry, Louie. We will leave it in the car."

My parents drop me off at the gym doors at 6:30, then go park the car. I head backstage so full of pre-show jitters I can barely see straight.

I'm wearing an orange T-shirt and jeans because bright colors and casual clothes help put the audience in a laughing mood.

To get my mind off my act, I pretend I'm Buster Keaton in his famous boxing lesson, where he keeps getting stuck in the ropes.

"Uh, Louie? What are you doing?" a voice behind me says.

I turn around and see Thermos, only she doesn't look anything like herself. She is wearing a poufy pink coat, a grumpy expression, and a big red bow. Her hair is long and curly.

"I'm going to do your act with you," she says. "For Nick."

She unbuttons the coat to reveal a ruffly red dress. "My mom made me wear this," she says. Her eyes dart around the room, making sure no one notices, and she pulls at her collar and scratches her shoulder like she's wearing the most uncomfortable clothing in the world.

"Wow," I say. "That's really nice of you." Thermos and I have never practiced together, but since the most likely outcome is failure, it should be okay. "You'll be my straight man. Just answer any questions I ask you, and no matter what happens, don't laugh!"

Thermos scowls

and gives the stink eye to Ryan Rakefield as he walks by. She tugs at the waist of her dress. I don't think not laughing will be hard for her.

Mrs. Adler comes over and pats Thermos on the shoulder. "You are a good friend." She gives my shoulder a squeeze. "Remember, Louie, you're offering the audience a gift. Present it from your heart and you'll do fine."

I nod my head as Mrs. Adler walks off to talk to Owen. Thermos looks as if she'd like to give the audience directions to the exit. Her lips are pressed together in a thin line. A swell of fear builds in my stomach.

We are the tenth act in the talent show, right before intermission. Thermos and I stand in the wings and watch the other acts, but Thermos won't take her coat off. Finally, the act right before ours takes the stage. It's Owen. His plate spinning has really improved.

For his finale, he gets five different plates going at the same time, in different directions. After a minute, my stomach spins, too. I close my eyes because the plates must be giving me reverse motion sickness.

When the announcer calls our names, my stomach still feels funny. And my ears don't work. His voice sounds tiny, like it's coming from miles and miles away.

I glance at Thermos. Her eyes are as round as Owen's plates. She looks like she wants to pull her coat over her head and disappear.

"Ready?" I ask.

Thermos nods. "I think so," she says, but it sounds like she's talking in a chicken voice.

"Okay," I say. "Let's go!"

I run out onstage, but don't hear her footsteps behind me. When I get there I'm alone. Off in the wings, Thermos is clutching her jacket to her chest and shaking her head. Maybe she never planned on helping me. Maybe this is her way of getting back at me.

My stomach lurches. I don't have to be good, I remind myself. I can fail spectacularly.

I turn and face the crowd. They look at me

expectantly. Can they tell I'm dying? Someone coughs and a cold sweat drips down my back. My stomach clenches.

Every bit of advice I ever got races through my head. From my parents, from Lou, from Mrs. Adler. Even from Ruby.

I look through the crowd. Ruby is sitting in the front row with my family and Ari's boyfriend, holding Dad's fancy camera. Mom said they'd leave it in the car. Why would they let Ruby hold it? She's probably going to film a ten-minute video of my knees.

Then Ruby shouts into the camera's microphone: "Ladies and gentlemen! Bannouncing the world's best comedian in the entire world . . . Louie Burger!"

People laugh, and an electric *zap* goes up my spine. I don't have to do my act for the whole room. I can do it for Ruby. I grab the mike and it's show-time!

"Hey there, boys and germs. Oops, I mean girls. I'm Louie Burger."

That gets a few chuckles, but Ruby laughs a deep belly laugh. I lean back on my heels and continue, even though my stomach is swirling. Maybe Mrs. Adler will be right about the stage fright leaving once my act gets going.

"I'm a pretty regular fifth grader," I say, "except for one thing. I'm not into sports. I wrote a little song about it for you. It's called 'Take Me Home from the Ball Game.'"

Take me home from the ball game.
I'm so bored I could cry.
I ate my peanuts an hour ago.
If I don't go home soon, I think I might die.
I would rather watch blades of grass grow.
It'd be more exciting, I think,
Than this "One, two, three strikes, you're out" stuff.
'Cause baseball stinks!

The audience laughs, but I can feel sweat starting to pour down my forehead. I'm ready for the part where the fear disappears.

"The only sport I'm into is competitive eating. How many hot dogs can a kid eat in two minutes? Now that's exciting. They serve *tofu* dogs in the school cafeteria. Did you ever notice that the word *tear* is in the middle of cafe-*tear*-ia? They know the food is so bad it'll make you cry."

I glance into the wings, and now Ryan and Jamal are standing next to Thermos. Ryan has a little smirk on his face. My spine stiffens. I'm ready to show him a thing or two about real comedy.

"Why do cafeterias serve foods with the word *surprise* in the name? Meat Loaf Surprise? Tuna Surprise? I don't want to be surprised by my lunch. It's never a good kind of surprise. You never bite into your meat loaf and say, 'Whoa! What a surprise! A forty-two-inch flat-screen TV!'"

The audience cracks up, but even better than that, I hear guffaws coming from backstage. I glance into the wings again and see Ryan laughing. For real. Even though my stomach still hurts, the rest of my stage fright is gone. I could tell jokes forever.

"I have a little problem when I eat too much," I tell everyone, and then I start to sing "The Burp Song." Because of the microphones, the burps reverberate around the gym, and the audience howls. On the last burp, I worry that more than air is going to come out of my stomach. I cover my mouth with my hand, but that makes people laugh even harder.

I peek down at Ruby. She's laughing so hard the

video's going to look like earthquake footage. My stomach twists. I bring my other hand to my mouth. I don't think I can talk anymore. Instead of my next bit, a geyser shoots up from my stomach. I spew chunks for real all over the stage.

Houston, we have a problem.

Fluffernutter soup. It's not a pretty sight.

At first, a few people in the back groan and laugh like they think it's a gag. But then I blow again, and my mom rushes to me. The houselights come up, and everyone murmurs in their seats.

"Are you okay?" asks Thermos, hurrying onstage from the wings. *Now* she unfreezes?

I nod weakly. I won't open my mouth again until I'm sure nothing will come out of it.

JoAnne brings the special powder and sprinkles it over the puddle on the stage. Mrs. Adler takes the microphone and announces the intermission, and my mom wipes me off with paper towels and tells me we're going home.

How barfmiliating.

Ladies and gentlemen . . . my first performance.

The Top Ten Things Worse than Throwing Up Onstage in Front of Two Hundred People

1. This is the first and last item on this list because I really can't think of anything worse than throwing up onstage. I don't want to be Louie Burger, the Boy Who Barfed.

(Although I guess I would be okay with it if someone wanted to pay me five million dollars to make my life story into a made-for-TV movie.)

WITH A BARF-BARF HERE AND A BARF-BARF THERE

(Insert "Old MacDonald Had a Farm" music here)

When we get home, Mom sends me straight to bed, and I actually feel grateful.

I also feel horrible. I mean really, really sick. My skin is clammy. My knees are weak and my stomach keeps heaving. Mom gives me a pail to keep by my bed.

Barf may not be as funny as I originally thought.

When morning comes, my stomach stops turning inside out, and I fall asleep and don't wake up until dinnertime. Ari brings me plain broth and Jell-O on a tray, which I get to eat in bed. The Jell-O tastes fluffmazing. (I'm trying out a new catchphrase in case barf and I never get back on speaking terms.) I never knew I was such a big Jell-O fan. It's almost as good as Marshmallow Fluff. Hey, I bet it would taste even better with Marshmallow Fluff.

Ruby walks in with the latest *Nutso* magazine and says, "I told Dad to buy this for you, since staying in bed is the most boringest thing in the whole world."

"Thanks," I say. That was pretty nice of Ruby. "When I feel better, want to play Magical Mystery Unicorns?"

"Unicornefinitely!" she says. I don't have the heart to tell her that her catchphrase needs work.

Ari and Ruby sit at the foot of my bed while I eat. Ari reads *Nutso* out loud, and we crack up at the comic strip "Winnie the Poo."

I laugh so hard it hurts. My stomach is sore from the barfing.

After Ari finishes the last page, Ruby says, "Want to watch the talent show video?"

"No way!" I shout. I almost knock my tray over.

Ari steadies it and puts it on the floor. I hide under my covers. "I don't ever want to see it. Throw it away. Erase it. Blast it with a laser!"

"You could still send it to Lou Lafferman," says Ari.

I shake my head. "It was a disaster," I say. "I didn't even fail the way I planned."

"You should still send it," says Ruby. "Everything before you threw up was funny."

"No way!" I really mean it. I did the talent show (at least until I threw up) and I'm proud of that, but I'm not ready for my big break. I need more practice.

Ari and Ruby take my tray back to the kitchen, and I uncover myself, lie down, and fall asleep.

When I wake up the next morning, my mom has already left for work. I feel okay, but Dad says I have to stay home from school for one more day, to be on the safe side. He sets me up on the couch with a pancake-and-Marshmallow-Fluff sandwich and last night's *Lou Lafferman.*

"I'm so proud of you," Dad says as he turns on

the TV. "You did it. You lived up to your end of the pact. That could be you someday." He points to Lou on the screen.

I take the remote from his hands and pause the TV. "Dad, what about your end of the deal?"

Dad gets a sheepish look on his face. "I don't know, Louie. I'm still trying to figure that out."

Before I can ask him if he wants a push, the phone rings.

It's Nick. I wonder if he knows about what happened at the talent show.

"Are you better?" he asks.

"Yeah," I say, "but I threw up onstage."

"I heard."

So word's gotten around.

"Don't feel bad. I barfed twenty-four times," Nick says. It makes my stomach feel sore again just to think about it. "Guess the Barf Brothers barfed again."

It feels good to hear him use our old nickname.

"Hey, Nick," I say. "You and Thermos did a great

job on your report. I never got to tell you. Kenji Okada is cooler than I realized."

"Thanks," he says. "Glad you noticed."

Nick and I talk for a while more, and for the first time in a long time it feels like I have my friend back.

After we hang up I watch a bunch of old episodes of *Lou* and take a nap. When I wake up, I realize there's someone else I need to call, so at 3:30, when I'm sure school is over, I pick up the phone and dial.

"Hello," I say. "May I speak to Thermos?"

"I'm sorry," the woman on the other end says. "There's no one here by that name."

"Oh." I double-check the school directory. Maybe I got a number wrong.

"Goodbye," she says.

"Wait!" I shout, realizing my mistake. "May I speak to Theodora?"

There is a pause on the other end of the line, then, "One moment. I'll get her."

"Hello?" Thermos says.

I clear my throat. "Uh, hi, it's Louie. I wanted to say thank you for doing the talent show with me."

"I didn't do it. I freaked out."

"Well, then, not thanks?"

Thermos makes a noise. I'm not sure what it is. Half laugh, half groan? "You're not welcome."

There is an awkward silence.

"But seriously," I say. "Thank you."

"Seriously," she repeats. "I didn't do anything."

This could go on all night. "You did! You came to the show. You were willing to be my partner even though I've been a jerk. I'm sorry I gave you such a hard time."

"You are?"

"I am. *Really.*"

"Okay," Thermos says. "I'll let you have a do-over. Want to ride bikes?"

I laugh. "At recess?"

"No! Right now. I can bike over to your house."

"Sure, but I don't know if Nick's allowed outside. His mom is extra careful about germs."

"That's okay," she says. "You and I can hang out alone sometimes, you know."

Huh. I never thought about that before.

I check with my dad, then say, "Come on over."

As soon as I hang up the phone, I realize I have a problem. Bike riding is basically a sport that is higher up off the ground. So when you fall, it's a lot worse. For example, your front tire could hit a unicorn that's lying in the middle of the driveway. The horn might go straight into your wheel and stop you dead in your tracks. Then you might fly over the handlebars and land in a kiddie pool filled with papier-mâché paste for a Fourth of July Statue of Liberty. Um. That didn't actually happen. *Really.*

And besides, if we ride bikes, Thermos might want to race or pop wheelies or ride no-handed or any number of things that could result in serious damage to my epidermis. But I can't say no. Not when Thermos and I are finally becoming, *gulp*, friends.

"My bike is buried in the garage," I tell her

when she gets to my house. I haven't used it since the unicorn incident that didn't actually happen. "It might be hard to get." There is a giant mess in there. My mom and dad are always planning to clean it out, but they never do.

"I can help." Thermos heads back toward the garage and I follow her. I punch in the key code and the door slides up to reveal a solid wall of stuff crammed so tightly together there isn't even a path to the inside.

"Whoa," says Thermos.

"I know," I say. "It could win the award for Messiest Garage on Earth."

"No," she says, pointing. "I mean those. Whoa!"

She's whoa-ing at the wire mailbox stands my dad made in the shape of Ruby, Ari, and me. He worked on those out on the driveway every weekend for the entire summer last year, but still never finished them. Whenever people walked by our house, they stopped to ask questions and a couple people even wanted to buy them.

"My dad made those."

"Your dad's an artist?" she asks. "Cool. My dad is an insurance analyst."

We burst out laughing, because we both know that's one of the most boring jobs ever.

"I think my bike might be in the back corner." I stand on tiptoes, trying to get a better look. "Behind those giant metal flower sculptures."

Thermos scratches her forehead. "We'll have to take everything out to get to it."

"We could do something else instead," I suggest. I'm sure Thermos doesn't want to clean out my garage any more than my parents do.

"No way," says Thermos. "Who knows what we might find in there! It's going to be awesome."

We start taking stuff out a piece at a time, but soon it's getting as messy outside the garage as it is inside, so Thermos and I decide to sort everything into different groups: Dad's art, gardening supplies, toys, mystery items, and trash. It takes us about two hours to get everything out of the garage. We find my bike halfway through, but the tires are deflated and we don't find the bike pump until we reach the very last corner.

"Your dad is really talented," she says, wandering through the miniforest of artwork on my driveway. There are mailbox stands, birdbaths, flower sculptures, scrap-metal birdhouses, a picnic table with no benches, a clock with no hands, candlesticks that don't match, and a bunch of different animal sculptures.

My dad used to have so much fun on the weekends. He never finished any of his projects, but he never worried about that. He cared more about making the art than the finished piece.

"What's going on here?" My dad comes outside with lemonade for me and Thermos. "I've never heard of kids cleaning out a garage for entertainment."

"Look at all your stuff, Dad."

"I forgot about these," he says, walking over to a bunch of birdhouse clocks. "And these." He runs his hand over the mailboxes.

"You should finish them," I tell him.

My dad studies me for a long time. "I'm going to start looking for a part-time job, Louie. But you're right. I could finish this stuff. Now that the garage is cleaned out, it'll be the perfect space for me to work in on the weekends."

I admire the empty garage. It is a great space. Now that it's clean, my mind can't help imagining what my stage would look like in there. My curtain could go against the back wall. And in front, there would be enough room to build a small set of bleachers. It would be the perfect place to rehearse, and to perform. For actual people.

I put my arm around my dad's waist. "Maybe we could share the garage."

Fluff Dictionary

Fluffabulous (adj.): better than fabulous.

Fluffcakes (n.): a pancake-and-Marshmallow-Fluff sandwich. The breakfast of fluffkids.

Fluffergy (n.): extra-super-high energy. You need a lot of *fluffergy* to play with Nick and Thermos.

Fluffernutter (n.): peanut butter and Marshmallow Fluff on white bread. The best sandwich in the world.

Fluffkids (n.): superfunny, supercool, and superinteresting kids. They might like sports and they might like comedy, but they love having fun.

Flufflarious (adj.): as funny as a Marshmallow Fluff pie in the face.

Flufflicious (adj.): the special delicious taste food gets when you add Marshmallow Fluff.

Flufftastic (adj.): amazing times fantastic plus Marshmallow Fluff. Squared.

THAT'S ALL, FOLKS!

So now that I have *two* best friends and an awesome new comedy club in my garage, fifth grade is almost back to perfect. I say *almost*, be-

cause my hero project was a bust. It's been two weeks, and everyone has gotten a letter back from his or her hero but me. Nick and Thermos both got signed pictures from Kenji Okada and Owen got Twinkie coupons. He wrote his letter to Hostess because his hero isn't alive anymore.

I should have chosen Archibald Query. At least I might have gotten free Fluff.

Lou's silence is such a bummer that I'm not even excited for the special Friday edition of male-bonding time my dad and I planned for tonight. He's letting me stay up late to watch *Lou Lafferman's Laff Nite* at its *real* time. He's been in a much better mood since he took a part-time job at Spiral Fine Arts Supply.

○ ○ ○

At 9:30, the doorbell rings. I'm in the kitchen unloading groceries. Dad took me shopping to buy ingredients for ice cream sundaes. Frozen yogurt is not a male-bonding-time snack so we got real ice cream, and tons of toppings, too—enough for about a hundred sundaes.

"Louie," my dad says, "I hope you don't mind, but I've invited some other people to join us to-night."

I bite my bottom lip. Male-bonding time is a two-person activity. You can't invite other people to join in.

"I must have a banana in my ear," I say, pre-tending to pull it out. "I don't think I heard that correctly."

"Well," he says, walking out of the kitchen and waving for me to follow him. "I thought it would be nice to include your mom, Ariella, and Ruby."

I am about to let him have it, because what he's describing is *family*-bonding time, and I already have plenty of that! But then my dad opens the front door.

". . . and Nick and Henry and Theodora," he says.

"Thermos," says Thermos, as she walks through the door.

"Right. Thermos," Dad repeats. "And Danny."

Henry is wearing his Superman cape and his pajamas. And Nick and Thermos have sleeping bags. I'm not even going to talk about Danny. It's too disgusting that my sister has a boyfriend. The only good part is that he's a boy. Also, he's a magician, so we have the whole performing thing in common. He told me he's jealous of my garage. I might rent it out to him.

I don't get what's going on. Why would my dad invite so many people to male-bonding time? I try to ask him, but he shoos us away so he can get everything set up for the viewing.

Nick, Thermos, and I sit down in my empty closet to play Don't Make Me Laugh. It's a board game. You have to do crazy things to try to crack your opponents up. The other players have to try to keep a straight face.

"I've never seen *Lou Lafferman* before," says Thermos.

I cannot believe it. Thermos is lucky she's friends

with me. First Fluffernutters and now *Lou Lafferman*. I'm introducing her to all the finer things in life.

"You'll love it," I say. "He's like me, only grown-up!"

My dad calls to us right as we finish the game. Thermos wins. She can flip her nostrils inside out. Flufftastic!

"Showtime!"

We race into the family room. Dad sets up TV trays with our sundae orders. I dig into chocolate ice cream with rainbow sprinkles, maraschino cherries, and extra Marshmallow Fluff!

Everybody finds a seat and Dad flips on the TV. *Lou Lafferman*'s about to begin, and Ruby starts making a racket. Even though I'm glad Nick and Thermos are here, I almost wish my dad and I were alone. I don't want Ruby to ask questions the whole time and laugh at the wrong parts.

"I don't want ice cream," she says. "I want popcorn with mustard."

"I'm not a restaurant," says my dad.

"I should get whatever snack I want!" Ruby shouts. "I'm the one who ta—"

"Shhh!" Ariella kicks Ruby in the shin.

My mom gives Ruby a warning look and pretends to zip her lips.

"Well I think I deserve a reward," says Ruby, crossing her arms over her chest. "And I still want popcorn."

The opening credits roll, and Dad turns the volume up. Lou walks out from behind the silver curtain and does a hysterical bit on toast. After the monologue, he walks over to his desk and the giant TV screen behind him pops up.

"We've got viewer videos for you tonight, folks," says Lou. "And this first one comes from a kid after my own heart. He's a young comedian named Lou. Unfortunately, he takes his act a little too seriously! Let's watch this clip of his fifth-grade talent show performance."

My heart pounds. I look around the room, and my parents beam at me. I pinch my arm. I must be dreaming.

"No way!" says Nick.

"I thought you didn't send it," says Thermos.

"Shhh!" I say as the clip starts to roll. I'm standing on the gymnasium stage singing "The Burp Song." My hand goes to my mouth, and then . . .

Up it comes.

Remembering that night makes my stomach shiver. I watch myself hurl a second time. Even though they blurred the actual throw-up, I think it is fair to say I've officially puked in front of 3.4 million people.

"Let's see that once more, folks," says Lou. The video rewinds, and everyone watches me barf again.

"You know, kid, they sell fake barf nowadays! It's not even that expensive. Get a paper route and you won't have to make it yourself anymore. But seriously"—Lou looks directly into the camera, as though he's talking only to me—"you've got a real future in comedy. I bet we'll see you on this stage one day. Bring your own cleaning service. We'll be right back, friends." Lou waves at the camera and the screen fades to a Denture-Fresh commercial.

"Aaaaaaaaahhhhhhhh!!!!" I scream. I jump up and down on the sofa. Nick and Thermos do, too. "I was on *Lou*! I was on *Lou*! I was on *Lou*!"

My dad stands up and says, "Jump on the floor, please. Off the furniture."

I leap off the couch, but I don't stop bouncing, even though I bang my knee and stub my toe on the coffee table. "I can't help it. I was on *Lou Lafferman*. But I don't understand how."

Ari stares at the ground. She won't make eye contact with me.

No way. "*You* sent it?" I ask her.

"Well, it was my idea. Dad figured out the right people to send it to. Ruby helped us write the letter."

"And I made the video of your throw-up," Ruby says, puffing out her chest. "I told you it was good enough to send."

"I think you guys are the best sisters in the world," I say, hugging them. "Though I may change my mind about that tomorrow."

"And what am I?" says Dad. "Mr. Nobody?"

I give him a hug.

"Ahem," says my mom.

I hug her, too, but do I have to hug everyone? I look at Nick, Thermos, Henry, and Danny, and shake my head. I believe the expression that applies is: *Not gonna happen.*

"Let's watch it again," says Thermos.

My dad rewinds the show. Thank goodness we

have every episode automatically set to be recorded. We watch me barf again.

As of tonight, fifth grade is turning out to be even better than perfect. It's fluffmazing with a side of flufftastic! Sometimes it pays to be a barfburger.

So there you have it, girlzillas and gentlemonkeys. (That's my new closer.)

The book is over. You can stop reading now.

Really. Stop.

Um, I believe the expression that applies here is: *That's all, folks!*

End of story.

Elvis has left the building.

There's a theme here, get it?

This is

THE END.

BOUNCE
BOUNCE
BOUNCE
BOUNCE
51
THE END

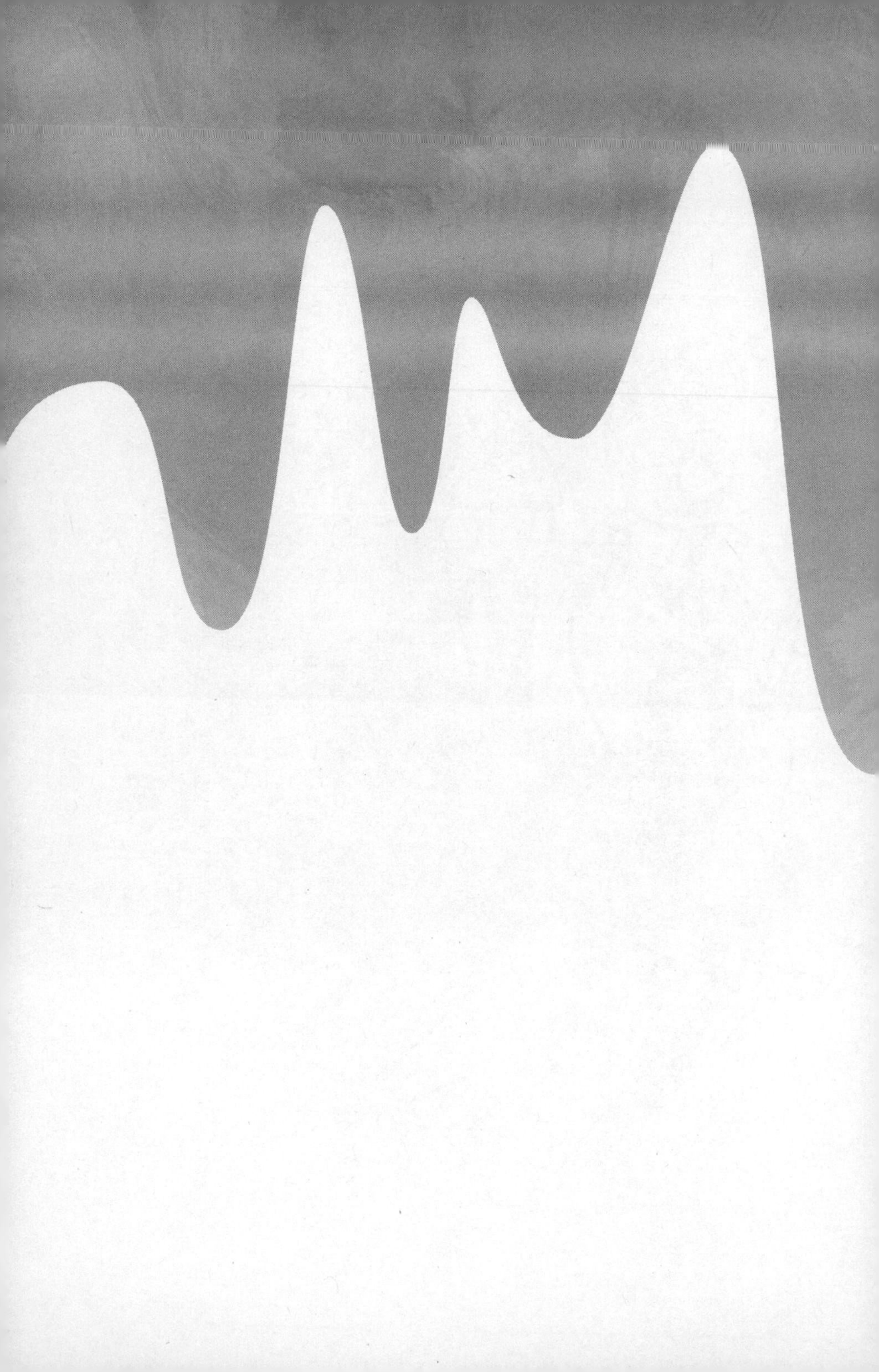

Acknowledgments

Thank you to Janine O'Malley and the amazing team who worked on this book with me.

To my wonderful family, Tigay side and Meyerhoff side, your love and support mean everything.

To Brenda Ferber, Carol Grannick, and Ellen Reagan, the critique group that midwived this book, our Mondays kept me sane and, more important, happy.

To Stephen Roxburgh, your insight and generosity saved the day.

To Jennifer Mattson, without you there would be no "fun factor."